NOVELS BY **BURT WEISSBOURD**

Cash and Callie Thrillers
Danger in Plain Sight
Rough Justice
Out of the Past

Corey Logan Thrillers
Inside Passage
Teaser
Minos

In Velvet
(a thriller set in Yellowstone National Park)

Danger in Plain Sight

"Here's what happens when you enter Mr. Weissbourd's world: You can't get out. You will be astonished not only by the colorful, playful, lethal characters, you will be hooked into a plot that laughs at whatever else you thought you were doing today. Callie and Cash, beauty and the beast, and the characters that swim through their world are each a gem of humanity observed."

—**David Field**, screenwriter and former head
of West Coast Production United Artists

"Weissbourd delivers a polished page-turner about terrorism, money laundering, and the price of sins rooted in avarice."

—*BlueInk Review*

"From the author of the brilliant Corey Logan Trilogy, *Danger in Plain Sight* is the latest thriller from Burt Weissbourd and his finest novel yet. Weissbourd has created an entire genre—*Seattle Noir*. Callie James and her son, Lew, are indelible characters. I devoured the novel in a single night–and I think you will, too."

—**Jacob Epstein**, writer and executive story editor
Hill Street Blues, writer *LA Law*

"A woman gets in touch with her inner action hero in this bracing thriller."

—*Kirkus Reviews*

Inside Passage

"A narrative that is relentlessly taut and exciting."

—*Foreword Reviews*

"*Inside Passage* hit all the hallmarks of a great read... Riveting story from the first paragraph."

—*Nightly Reading*

"The family dynamics and insights to human behavior had me reeling.... Juicy, fascinating stuff."

—*The (Not Always) Lazy W*

"*Inside Passage* is a great thriller and the restaurants you include as part of the story: Canlis, El Gaucho, Tulio, Queen City Grill, Wild Ginger, are all very sexy places. You really captured our city!"

—**Scott Carsburg**, James Beard award winner
and legendary Seattle chef

"I got completely hooked on *Inside Passage*'"

—**Nancy Guppy**, host of *Art Zone* on Seattle Channel

Teaser

"A stunning, fast-paced thriller."

—*Roxy's Reviews*

"Burt Weissbourd is such a great writer… Such a great book!"

—*So I Am a Reader*

"Weissbourd, a seasoned screenwriter and film producer, has the mechanics down pat. Teaser is a fun, action-filled ride."

—*Foreword Reviews*

"Weissbourd's stellar writing, memorable characters and an extremely well-crafted narrative never disappoint."

—*Discerning Reader*

Minos

In Velvet

"This thrilling novel has a breathless pace that combines science and nature to create nail-biting tension."

—*Foreword Reviews*

"*In Velvet* left me breathless, a bit contemplative, and completely satisfied."

—*Manic Readers*

"Weissbourd's writing reminds me of the great Raymond Chandler mysteries."

—**John McCaffrey**, *KGB Bar Lit Mag*

"*In Velvet* is a thrill from start to finish!"

—*Closed the Cover*

MINOS

MINOS

BY BURT WEISSBOURD

BLUE CITY PRESS
ISLIP, NY

RARE BIRD
LOS ANGELES, CALIF.

The Temple of Apollo at Delphi, where Apollo's Oracle, a priestess, was consulted by Greek and foreign heads of state, dignitaries, military leaders, and common people before they made an important decision. She was the most revered oracle, and among the most powerful women in the classical world.

THIS IS A GENUINE RARE BIRD | BLUE CITY PRESS BOOK

Rare Bird Books
6044 North Figueroa Street
Los Angeles, California 90042
rarebirdbooks.com

Blue City Press
62 West Bayberry Road
Islip, New York 11751

Printed in the United States

10 9 8 7 6 5 4 3 2 1

Publisher's Cataloging-in-Publication data

Names: Weissbourd, Burt, author.
Title: Minos : a Corey Logan thriller / by Burt Weissbourd.
Description: First Hardcover edition. | A Vireo Book. | New York [New York] ;
Los Angeles [California] : Rare Bird Books, 2016.
Series: The Corey Logan Trilogy
Identifiers: ISBN 978-1-942600-40-4
Subjects: LCSH Preparatory schools—Fiction. | Psychiatrists—Fiction. | Mythol-
ogy, Greek—Fiction. | Murder fiction. | BISAC FICTION/General | FICTION /
Mystery & Detective / General.
Classification: LCC PS3623.E45925 M56 2016 | DDC 813.6—dc23.

To Kenneth Millar

THE MINOTAUR

(MINOTAUROS, "THE BULL OF MINOS")

When Minos claimed the Cretan throne, he prayed to Poseidon to send him a sign as proof of his right to reign. At once, a dazzling snow-white bull (the Cretan Bull) emerged from the sea. Though Minos had promised to sacrifice this bull to Poseidon, he found it so beautiful that he sent it to join his herd and sacrificed another bull instead.

Poseidon, enraged, made Minos' wife, Pasiphae, fall in love with the wondrous, white bull. She confessed her unnatural passion to Daedalus, the master craftsman, who made a hollow wooden cow with wheels concealed in its hooves. Pasiphae climbed inside it wanting to mate with the great white beast. Daedalus wheeled it to the meadow where the bull was grazing. The bull mounted the wooden cow, and Pasiphae gave birth to a horrible monster, the Minotaur, a creature with the head of a bull and the body of a man. Pasiphaë nursed him, but he grew fierce and wild, devouring men for sustenance.

Horrified and ashamed, Minos consulted the Oracle at Delphi about how he might hide his terrible secret. The Oracle told him to have Daedalus construct a gigantic labyrinth, at the center of which he could conceal the Minotaur.

PROLOGUE

Minos admired his work. The scar was still there, if you looked closely, and yes, a thin line ran up from his partially closed eye, across his forehead. But now, there was the birthmark, a scarlet bloom, covering part of his left cheek. The way he did it, the birthmark was darkest in the center where it covered his scar. That way, the scar tissue was not so noticeable under the deep-purple inkblot, staining his cheek from lip to brow. He studied the bottles on the long table, dabbing his swabs in one, then another. Like a painter, Minos made adjustments on his palette before extending the birthmark downward.

He applied the eyeliner, then the shadow. These he used because it pleased the Master. Minos thought he looked fancy, even gaudy, but that was fine if it made the Master happy. The Master found beauty in unlikely things.

He looked again in the mirror and adjusted the overhead Halogens so that his face was fully lit. He liked how his curly black hair, a handsomely crafted wig, rested naturally on his head. Satisfied, he raised his long fingers and framed his face. Minos stood and waited, poised. When he felt steady and easy, even silky on the inside, he began his slow, silent dance. Minos' fingers curled into fists, finding their marks in the air, uncurling again. His fingers moved deftly, making shapes in the air, until the extended forefinger of each hand settled just above his temples, curling forward. Then he swayed his body, graceful and deliberate.

He was back in ancient Crete, where every year there was a sacrifice of a boy, a surrogate for Minos, the Bull King. The boy reigned for a day then danced through the five seasons—lion, goat, horse, serpent and bull calf—as Zagreus, Zeus's son by Persephone, had done when fleeing from the Titans.

Zeus had intended Zagreus to be his heir, and he entrusted him, like the infant Zeus in Cretan myth, to the care of the Titans. Hera, Zeus's jealous wife, convinced the Titans to kill the child. When they tried to seize him, the divine infant showed great courage, transforming alternatively into a lion, a horse, a goat, a serpent, even a bull, as he fled in an attempt to escape. But the Titans grabbed his horns and feet and tore him apart, devouring him. Upon discovering their crime, Zeus struck the Titans dead with thunderbolts, turning them to ash. It is said that from the ashes of the Titans, containing the divine flesh they had just eaten, rose mortals, who were partly evil and partly divine.

Minos smiled into the mirror. Remembering this poignant story of how Zeus, Minos the Bull King's father, had created humankind gave him new energy and increased the intensity of his dancing. Minos liked his dance, it reminded him of who he was and what he was capable of.

As he danced, his body changed. The heaviness and the worries lifted. Then, he was loose. Out from under. Riding the wave. He danced his silent dance, watching in the mirror, until the change was complete. When he was satisfied, Minos framed his face with his forefingers again. He bowed slightly, then adjusted his posture, stooping, just a little, so his shoulders disappeared. Minos affected a slowness, a tentativeness to his movements. He tilted his head down, just barely, so he wouldn't make eye contact. He practiced his walk, bowing after, like a street performer, then put on his long, black leather greatcoat over black pants, a black turtleneck and his favorite black suspenders. It was almost time, he knew, but Minos checked his pocket watch anyway. He liked the feel of it in his palm. His father had carried this same silver watch on its tarnished silver chain. Yes, it was time to leave.

He stood in front of the mirror, still. When he was ready—when he felt just so—Minos turned off his Skytron Halogens, his Remcraft Baci mirror, and shuffled out into the world.

CHAPTER ONE

Sara walked the wide corridor at her school, The Olympic Academy, frightened. There was great danger, she was sure of it. And none of the gods was listening. She ran her fingers across the never-to-be-touched Renaissance tapestry hanging on the Olympic Academy's Italian stone wall. Maybe they were waiting, watching what she'd do.

At fifteen and a half, her face still showed traces of acne. It would be a beautiful face one day, she was often told, but it wasn't so beautiful now, not to her anyway. She thought her face was scrawny and pasty, her features too delicate, too weak.

Her willowy body was changing, every day it seemed, and the one good thing was that her breasts had gotten big enough to notice. Her black hair with its shiny red streaks was good too, she had to say. She kept it cut short, so it wouldn't get in her way. Sara fingered the sharp points on her spiked leather collar. More and more, she liked sharp things. And she liked the way the silver looked with the black clothes she wore.

The bathroom was quiet, set back at the midpoint of the hallway. Inside, Sara checked the stalls, then locked the bathroom door. The room was small, only two stalls, but there was a big open space, big enough, anyway. She double-checked that the door was locked. Making sure. The door was oak, Zeus's wood, which was good. She rubbed the door, calling on Zeus, the thunderer, to help her. She carried a bulging canvas shoulder bag, which she set in the sink before checking herself out in the mirror.

With the double-edged blade of her ancient dagger, her Athame, Sara scratched a circle in the hardwood floor. A magic circle, it would keep her safe. Then, in the circle, a five-pointed star. Sara liked how, as she carved, the black wooden handle stayed steady in her hand. She lay her Athame on the oak floor near the edge of her circle. At each of the points of the star, she set a candle. She took three more candles from her worn canvas shoulder bag, and, deliberately, Sara set two on the windowsill and one on the shelf in front of the mirror. When the candles were lit, she took her bag and stood in the center of the circle.

From her bag, she took a vial of water. Pointing her first and second fingers at the water, she said, "I exorcise thee, creature of water, by the living God." Then she lifted the vial of salt, and pointing her fingers she went on, "I exorcise thee, creature of earth." Then, casting the salt into the water, "Grant that this salt may make for health of body and this water for health of soul, and that there may be banished from the place where they are used every power of adversity and every illusion and artifice of evil." And then, sprinkling the water around her circle, "In the Name which is above every other name, I exorcise all influences and seeds of evil..." When Sara was finished, she set down the salt and the water, safe now, in her circle, ready to begin. She lowered her head, hoping against hope that this time, she'd find a way to reach Theseus. She had to—yes, she had to—she knew that much.

From the floor, Sara raised her Athame above her head. Softly she whispered, "I am the priestess, the vestal virgin. I pray to the Oracle of Apollo, the serpent slayer. I must find Theseus. I need him now. I call on the Oracle to help me find him. I need him now..." From her bag she took a vial of wine, honey, chopped cheese and meal—her homemade ambrosia, the divine nectar of the gods. She drank it down, letting it run down her chin, her neck, as she called, "Blue-haired Poseidon, master of ships and stallions, you who sired him, lead me to Theseus. I call on Theseus. The Beast is rising. I need him now..." As she called, Sara twirled, dancing in ever-widening circles, her Athame held high.

Lost in her magical dance, Sara twirled and twirled, arms above her head, whispering, "Sacred Oracle of Apollo, lord of the silver bow, I pray you help me find Theseus..." She was repeating Theseus' name for a third time when her Athame hit a candle on the windowsill. The candle, which was set in a small glass container, fell against the green and red paisley curtain. The fire was instantaneous. As Sara chanted and twirled, the curtain ignited, from sill to ceiling. Sara turned on the water in the sink, splashing it with her hands toward the smoke and flames. The wooden wall behind the curtains was blackening now. As she hurried to fill a glass with water, the smoke alarm on the ceiling went off—a deafening, incessant shriek. Sara shrunk to the floor, hands over her ears, chanting, "Theseus, hear me now. I need you. I call you now. The Beast is rising. I summon you. I cannot stand alone…

When they broke down the door, Sara was in her circle, still chanting. Tears spilled down her cheeks. The point of her Athame was stuck in the floor, at the center of her circle. The wall had caught fire, and smoke covered the ceiling. When the fire was finally out, Owen Sentor, the acting dean at the Olympic Academy, quietly asked, "Sara, what are you doing?"

Sara dried her tears with the shiny black sleeve of her jersey. "Summoning the Oracle," she replied, still scrunched up on the floor.

"I beg your pardon?" His left eyelid was twitching, just barely. Little red spots were starting to show on the left side of his face.

"There's danger. I need help." She took a slow breath. "I can't reach Theseus. I thought Apollo's Oracle might help."

"Sara, this is a school restroom. This is not Delphi."

She raised her head. "Don't I know it. They pay attention at Delphi."

◆◆◆

Half an hour later Sarah was still in Dean Sentor's waiting room, wondering what it would take to make her magic work. The witchcraft, which was new to her, was necessary, she thought, because there was danger, especially at school. And today, she felt it more than ever. In her magic circle, she was safe and could do her work. The real work though— and this part she just knew in the way she knew certain things, which was all the way to the marrow of her bones—was contacting Theseus. She'd reached the Oracle before, and she was certain Poseidon would help if he could. After all, he was Theseus' father. One of them, anyway. Still, she couldn't even find him. *And no one was helping.* Maybe Poseidon, the storm maker, was angry. If he was, she'd have to figure out why. Perhaps the Oracle would help her choose the proper sacrifice. She didn't think she could kill a goat or a lamb though.

She crossed her long legs, adjusting her position on the hard, waiting-room couch. With her finger, she traced the pentagram tattooed on her ankle. She smelled something sweet—chocolate, a candy bar, she thought—and found a piece of a Snickers squished between the cushions. She decided to leave it where it was.

Sara was thinking how she'd try reaching the Oracle again after school, in Interlaken Park—how she'd cast a circle at her special spot—when her father arrived. Dr. Jim Peterson was in a hurry. He walked in with his silver-haired head held high and a friendly smile.

He hugged her after he came in. "What's up?" he asked his daughter.

"I needed help. I tried to reach the Oracle and find Theseus."

"Where?"

"In the school bathroom."

"Where?"

"You know, the little unisex one off the main hall." Her thin eyebrows angled down. "I locked the door."

"You couldn't wait?" Jim took an inhaler from his pocket, anticipating.

"I was scared."

He put his arm around her. "Honey, we agreed you'd do this on your own time."

Sara shrugged. "It gets worse."

Her father made a how-could-it-get-worse face. He took a burst from his inhaler, timing it in the way that only came from long experience with breathing difficulties.

"You see I cast a protective spell, to be safe while I was looking for him. So I lit my candles and made this really nice circle with my Athame. Anyway, when I was really—you know—into it, almost ready, I knocked over a candle, and the curtains caught fire."

"Sara—" Jim caught himself, took deliberate breaths, as the door to Owen Sentor's office opened. "Hello, Owen," he said, raising his head.

"Jim," Owen nodded, grim-faced. "Please come in." He held open the door to his cluttered office. Owen motioned for them to sit on his old corduroy couch. "I'll get right to the point," he explained. "I'm asking Sara to take some time off—"

"Suspended? Are you—?"

Her father put a hand on her arm, shushing her.

"Sara, you need help. Professional help. When you've gotten it, we'll talk about how you might become part of the community again." Owen looked at her. "I'm sorry, Sara, but we've done what we can. Now it's up to you. Do you have anything to say?"

Sara stood. Her eyes narrowed as she stared at her dean. "May the wrath of mighty Poseidon, the earth-shaker, make your days long and filled with shame." She raised her middle finger as she walked out his door.

Jim raised his inhaler to his mouth again.

CHAPTER TWO

The old oak table was messy but the rest looked okay. Which was something—what kind a shrink had his office over a Chinese takeout place that smelled like fermenting fish sauce? At least that's what Sara was thinking when she walked into Abe Stein's office. She sank into his worn, cherry-colored leather chair, wondering if he was as weird as she was. He was big, like a bear with a beard, she thought. A wise old bear that didn't care how he looked. And everything about him, even his face, was kind of wrinkly—yeah, he looked more like a shaggy bear than a psychiatrist. Which was a plus, as far as she was concerned. It wouldn't hurt if he got a new sport coat. She could see where his pipe—at least she assumed it was a pipe since he had the charred, chewed-on things strewn all over his desk—had burned a hole in the pocket of his tweed jacket.

The bear shrink just sat there, staring at her. What was he waiting for, she wondered? Did he think she'd pitch a fit or something? She could wait, too. It might be a good way to go, actually. The only use she had for a shrink was if he could get her in touch with Theseus, which definitely wasn't part of any head-shrinker's program. Un-unh. Never. She wondered if even Zeus, the king of heaven and earth, could move a shrink. Probably not. She'd bet he could zap one with a lightning bolt, though. Or turn him to stone. Yeah, that would be good.

He raised his pipe.

"Isn't there some kind of no smoking deal?" Sarah asked, pulling her nose ring, wondering if he'd wince or shift his butt. Nothing.

"My landlord lives in Hong Kong."

She wanted to smile. Smoky the shrink. Instead, she shrugged, who cares? When it was lit, Dr. Stein threw the match into a big stone bowl. She could already smell his nasty smoke.

"What happened at school?" he eventually asked.

Well, he got right to it, she had to give him that. And his voice was soft and friendly. Unless it was some kind of shrink trick. Sara looked him in the eye. "There's danger. I called on the Oracle of Apollo, the keeper of truth, to reach Theseus. I need his help."

"What kind of danger?"

"The Beast is rising. Only Theseus can stop him."

Abe took that in. "And the fire?"

"It's way too scary, what's been going on. So I had to make my magic circle, cast a protective spell. Anyway, I was really into it, and I accidentally knocked over a candle with my Athame." All of this said matter-of-fact. When she saw that he was confused, she took her Athame out of her canvas bag, showing him the double-edged dagger.

He nodded, thanks. Then, after a beat, "You know, two times I've set fires here in the office." Abe smiled, remembering. "Without meaning to."

"No kidding?" She leaned in, interested in this. "If you lie, I'm outta here."

"Really. I'm serious. I don't practice magic. But, as you can see, I'm a pipe smoker. What I'll do is, I'll light my pipe, then toss the match in the wastebasket, or in the ashtray. Every now and then, I think the match is out, and it isn't. Next thing I know, my desk is on fire, or smoke is pluming out of the waste basket."

Sara smiled, just barely, for the first time. "That's why you have that big old bowl of an ashtray, huh?"

"Exactly." He nodded again, plainly enjoying her quickness.

"How can we get this over with?" she asked then, taking advantage of his good mood.

"That depends." Abe sat forward, taking her question seriously. "Why are you here?"

Her eyebrows rose, followed by her eyes. "Gimme a break."

"Okay. You're here because your father made you come. And he made you come because your school said you had to have treatment before you would be re-admitted."

"So far so good." This guy was smart, and tricky. But he seemed to like her, she could tell. Which surprised her a lot. People didn't usually like her too well. Her dad said she needed to make a better first impression. What he really meant was she should lose the spiked collar. She fingered a spike, thinking about it.

"I propose another alternative," Abe interrupted her musing. "I suggest that you consider the possibility that I could actually help you."

"With what?"

"What would you like help with?"

Sara just snorted.

Abe frowned. "I'm not kidding."

"No fucking way." Her face tightened, sorry she'd let that slip.

He waited.

She better say something, get this back on track. What worried her most was that he would get in her way. Slow her down. Try and help with something he'd never, ever get. She hoped he'd give up on talking and just give her some medicine, which she'd never take, and ask to see her once a week. She could manage that. "Help me how?"

"What kind of help do you want?"

She decided to get it over with. Wake him up. "Mister, how about you help me fight the Beast? He's rising. He'll kill soon. I need a hero. I need more power. I need Theseus. Can you help me find him? Can you reach Poseidon, or Apollo? Huh? You up to that?" Shit. That ought to blow him off.

"Tell me more," he said softly.

Tricky bear shrink. Okay. Let's see. You want more—chew on this, shrinko. Sara closed her eyes, mumbling softly. She could smell the Beast; she could feel the scary things, coming on. Sara let them come, then speaking louder so he could hear, "Wild, shaggy Centaurs ravage the women at the wedding feast of their Lapith friends. Drunken, rampaging Maenads take Pentheus for a wild beast and rip him limb from limb. His mother, Abave, tears off his head. Seven maids and seven boys, Helene children, are given each great year, a sacrifice to the Minotaur in Crete. Furies walk in darkness, with bat's wings, writhing snakes for hair and eyes that weep tears of blood. The Beast is rising. He'll kill soon. No one will listen. Not Apollo, bearer of light, not Poseidon, the horse-father, nor even all-knowing Zeus."

"How can I help?"

Sara ignored him, crying softly. It was back, the thing in her gut, like she was passing small, sharp-edged stones. The bear shrink had tricked her. All she wanted to do was get him off her back. "You can't help me. You're making it worse," she whispered. Her face was pinched. She raised her Athame from her lap.

Abe stood, puzzled.

Sara was up, whispering. "Oh great and patient Oracle. I pray to you. Let me kneel on Apollo's altar, your devoted priestess. I summon you. There is no time. Hear me now. Please—"

Abe came behind her, holding her arm, taking her Athame, leading her back to her chair.

No one was listening. Why? Why was he touching her? Sara twisted her arm free and punched him in his big stomach. Then she stood still, silent, feet planted.

Abe stepped back.

Sara melted into the big leather chair, her feet underneath her, her head bowed, and her arms wrapped around her knotted stomach. When she finally raised her head to speak, her voice came out softly, "You can't help me, and you don't know who can." Then she lowered her head, hugging herself tightly.

Abe stood above her. "Let me try, Sara. I'd like to try." His furrowed brow formed a V as he waited for her to look up. "You may be surprised."

◆◆◆

The swing was a favorite spot for Billy Logan-Stein and his mom, Corey Logan. Neither of them could say exactly how it happened, but weather permitting—and their tolerance for foul weather was high—the two of them ended up on that creaky front porch swing maybe twice a week, spring, summer and fall. Today was a cloudy April day, and an on-again-off-again drizzle had left the sidewalks slick and gunmetal grey.

Corey was sitting beside her son, slowly rocking. She'd asked him a question, and he was thinking it over. They had the same black hair, parted in the middle, though hers was cut short and his was tied back in a little ponytail. She wore a blue sweater and form-fitting jeans, which is what she almost always wore. Today, she wore a pea coat—the same coat she'd worn at sea, running from Nick Season almost two years ago.

Billy liked long flannel shirts worn unbuttoned over a tee shirt and well-worn jeans. Corey had a patch of freckles on her nose that crept onto her cheeks when she smiled. Billy's face was darker, and she thought, darkly handsome, even when he was frowning, as he was now.

Billy's frown softened as he turned toward his mom. "Sara kind of freaked out," he explained, in response to her question about the fire at school.

"Is she okay?"

"She's not hurt, if that's what you mean. But she's not exactly okay either."

"How's that?"

"She's got this idea that we're all in danger, and she keeps talking about how these Greek Gods are supposed to help her. It's kind of weird."

"Greek Gods—like Poseidon or Zeus?"

"Yeah. Like in the myths. You know—"

Corey nodded. When Billy was younger, she'd told him the same myths her Greek mother had told her. "That is weird."

"She got suspended."

"I'm sorry. I like her and her dad."

"She's sort of a friend. I mean she's younger, but she's unpopular. I mean I'm unpopular, but she's like poster-child unpopular, which is even worse. The popular kids make fun of her. And they can be really mean." He nodded, ruefully, when his mom frowned. "I like her okay, and she's friends with Randy. So we kind of all stick together, you know, look out for her." Billy nodded again; he knew high school life. And then, an afterthought, "She sometimes reminds me of Maisie."

Corey remembered Maisie, vividly—how she was before, and after, she was kidnapped by Teaser. "How so?"

"Really smart, fast…" And after a beat, "How's Maisie doing? When I see her, she's still so quiet."

"You know your dad can't really talk about that. It's no secret, though, that he's still working with her. What I do know is that she'll be back next fall. Her mom's home schooling her. I ran into Amber at this parent food drive deal, and she told me that Maisie will be in your senior class."

"That's good…really good. Aaron and his family will be back from China then, too. I mean I really like hanging with Amy's friends, but they're seniors already and they'll be gone next year. It'll be good for me to have Maisie and Aaron around, especially if Amy's gone."

"I get that." And shifting gears, "Who says you're not popular?"

"Hey, I'm your son—I know what I know."

"I don't get it."

"When you were in prison, I got drugs for the popular kids. I've told you about that."

Corey nodded.

"When I stopped. They got pissed off. They never forgave me. And now I'm with Amy, who used to hang with them. I think Dave, the ringleader, has a crush on her. So now they routinely give me and my friends a hard time."

"Can I do anything?"

Billy smiled at his mom, imagining her bracing Dave or Russ. "No, we're okay. We pretty much ignore them."

"You're popular with Amy," Corey remarked, thinking Billy was more and more like Abe, the way he was so realistic about his life, and the way he could talk about it.

"Amy's cool," Billy said, smiling now and rocking. He was taller than Corey, and still gangly. His long arm was draped over the back of the porch swing, around her back. He touched her far shoulder, and when she turned that way, surprised, they laughed, a private joke between them. "I really like her."

"How are you two doing?" she eventually asked.

"She wants to go out."

"What exactly does 'go out' mean?" Corey ran her hand through her short, black hair. There was a braided red and black bracelet tattooed on her wrist.

"It means we see each other a lot. You know, lunch, after school, even at night on the weekends."

"Sounds serious." Corey watched his face. Billy's first, and last, girlfriend, Morgan, had ended their relationship six months after her family moved to New York City less than a year ago.

"I dunno. We've only been together—what?—it's not even three months."

"I'm sure she's had her eye on you for quite a while. She was just waiting for you and Morgan to break up."

"You think?"

"Yeah, that's what I think, and even if you factor in that I'm your mom, I'll bet I'm right."

Billy smiled. "It's not always, well, a good thing, to have a mom who's so sure of everything."

"Fair enough…so what's worrying you?"

"Well she's had lots of boyfriends, and she might lose interest."

"Why would she do that?"

"I'm not so…you know."

Corey took a beat, putting it together. Okay, Mom. "You mean you're not as experienced as she is?"

"I guess."

When Billy was uncomfortable, he got vague, monosyllabic. "Listen. I went out with guys who weren't as experienced as I was, and the ones that I kept seeing were the ones that didn't pretend it wasn't so."

His black eyebrows tilted down. "How do you do that?"

Corey leaned in, pleased that he was asking her about this. Pleased, too, that he was smart enough to know she could help. "Tell her. You can even ask questions about what she likes."

"Are you kidding?"

"Hey. Let her take the lead. It's just the two of you, you know. No one else cares." Her smile, when it came, was open and warm.

He thought about that. "Huh," was all he offered, along with another tap to her far shoulder.

◆◆◆

At the end of his day, Abe returned phone calls. He rubbed his thumb over a well-worn spot on the old oak desk and dialed Jim Peterson's number at work. Abe believed the groove in his desk had been worn while he waited for doctors. As he held for Dr. Peterson, he was thinking about Sara, how she was so sensitive, even hypersensitive; Sara didn't miss much. And the mythological universe she'd constructed was, at first glance, both orderly and detailed. No small accomplishment. Still, he had no idea why she'd built it, or what purpose it served. He hoped to answer those questions. He couldn't do that, though, without her help. And why would she ever want to help him unless she thought he could help her? She didn't think that now; he knew that much. After holding for a very busy receptionist and an even busier nurse who asked if he was waiting for "Doctor," he explained that he, too, was a doctor returning Dr. Peterson's call, and Abe was put through right away.

"Jim, Abe Stein," Abe said. They'd had patients in common, and though they didn't know each other well, Abe liked and respected Jim. He was sure Jim wouldn't have sent Sara to see him if the feeling wasn't mutual.

"Nice to talk with you, Abe, sorry about the circumstances. I'm worried. I'd appreciate your take on Sara."

"My take?" Abe was wary—something about the way some doctors assumed they were part of some special club, that Abe would just tell him about Sara, his daughter, Abe's patient.

"I'll level with you, Abe. I'm okay with the black clothes, the Wicca, the spells. I've learned to live with the piercings, the pentagrams, even the tattoos. And Lord knows, since she was a child, I've encouraged her interest in Greek mythology. But this is different. She's depressed. She's become uncommunicative and reclusive. In the past few weeks, it's gotten worse. To her, these Greek stories are becoming real. And setting a fire at school is a felony. Help me out here. I'm lost. I don't know what to do."

"I'm not sure what you're asking."

"Can you help her? What's the matter with her?"

Abe hesitated. "Jim, you're putting me in an awkward position. If I'm going to treat Sara—and I suggested we meet three times a week—I can't have side conversations with you. If you want to come in, I'll talk with Sara first and work out what I can and can't say."

"Cut me a little slack here, Abe. I know how this works."

Abe was quiet. "I'll do my best to help Sara," he eventually offered.

"Okay. I know. That's why she's seeing you."

"Jim, I need time with her. I can't say yet how long. I can only help her if you give us time and room."

"I'm sorry if I was out of line, I'm just—I'm just upset, and honestly, sometimes I'm so worried it's hard to bear."

"I understand." And he did. Abe could still see Sara—she was imprinted, indelibly, in his mind—waving her Athame, calling on the Oracle of Delphi to help her. It was as if she'd embraced, no, ingested, Greek mythology, then added a dash of the occult. And now, she was insisting that worrisome aspects of her modern life were driven by the strict rules and harsh consequences of the ancient Greek Myths.

Abe could hear Jim, taking a slow breath, using his inhaler. "Take what time you need, Abe," he eventually said, "But please work out with Sara some way to keep me in the picture. Okay?"

"I'll try."

"Thanks for your help." Jim said.

"I haven't helped yet," Abe wanted to say. "And I'm not sure I can." Instead, he said, "I'll do my best."

Abe set down the phone, wondering why Sara had retreated to a world that existed, what?—he checked a mythological timeline. It estimated that Theseus was born in 1273 BC—more than 3,200 years before her father was born.

◆◆◆

Minos still kind of liked this stretch of Broadway. Even though it had changed, lost its funky, one-of-a-kind character. Even though the best places, like Meteor Man, were gone. Change is usually for the worse, Minos thought. But he liked how he still knew his way around both sides of the street: he knew where to find wallets, cheap jewelry, funny T-shirts, pagan trinkets, CDs, cigarette cases, dirty magazines, even exotic knives.

He knew the stores for rich kids, like the Gap or Urban Outfitters. What was bothering him then? What it was, he decided, was that he missed the old Broadway Market. He missed the candy store, and the newsstand with papers from all over the world. Most of all, he missed the men's underwear place, Meteor Man, and the Rubber Rainbow Condom Company which used to be upstairs and was very cool. He wasn't sure why he missed these things, but he did. The Oxygen Bar had been upstairs, too, but Minos thought it was, at best, some kind of joke. Breathing fancy air was a fool's game.

What he still liked about this stretch of Broadway—the one big thing—he realized, were the people. Especially the kids. Weekends there were always kids, passing through, checking it out. All kinds of kids. That's what he liked, yeah. He thought the kids from everywhere else tried to look like they belonged here, and sometimes that made them weirder looking than the real street kids. There were ordinary people, too—tourists, parents, suburban kids, local high school kids, college kids, shoppers. In fact, statistically speaking, most of the people cruising Broadway were mainstream. But it wasn't their place, and they knew it. That was what drew them here. The street folk set the tone. Leather, metal, piercings and tattoos meant to shock, and, always the hair, the wild and crazy hair. Some days, it was like getting a little glimpse of the marketplace from Star Wars, some of the kids were so wonderfully weird-looking. Which was good for Minos. He fit in. He belonged here. He was the genuine article, the real deal. Minos was a grown-up version of a wonderfully weird-looking kid. Grown-up on the outside, anyway. On the inside, he was like the other kids, more or less. He smiled, liking how he could feel old and young at the same time. This was a good place for it, too. Often, he would sit at one of the little tables in the coffee shop and watch the kids go by.

Minos sat, checking out a handsome boy with green hair. Before long, he was thinking about the boy he'd lost. He thought he might turn green with envy, remembering how Minos, the Cretan Bull King, had gone to the Delphic Oracle to find his missing son. Unbeknownst to the Bull King, his son, Glaucus had gone into the cellar at the palace, where he'd fallen into a great jar of honey, head downward, and drowned. The Oracle had said, "A marvelous creature has been born amongst you: whoever finds the true likeness for this creature will also find the child." The Bull King learned that a heifer-calf had been born that changed its colors three times a day—from white to red and from red to black. He brought his soothsayers to the palace and Polyeidus of Argos said, "this calf resembles nothing so much as a ripening blackberry," and Minos sent him to find Glaucus.

Polyidus found Glaucus drowned in the jar of honey. Minos demanded Glaucus be brought back to life and locked Polyeidus in a tomb with Glaucus and a sword. A serpent approached the boy's corpse and Polyeidus killed it with the sword. Another snake came and seeing its mate dead, this snake slithered off and returned with an herb that brought its mate back to life. Polyeidus used this same herb to miraculously resurrect Glaucus.

Minos loved that story—the serpent, the resurrection of the boy, and especially the part about the wondrous heifer-calf. He could bring that heifer-calf here, to the new market, Minos was thinking. The kids would stop by and watch it, pet it, maybe get stoned and hang out, *ooing* and *ahing* as the calf changed colors. Never knowing its meaning.

Today, he had business, the Master's business. He stood up, then began walking his walk, keeping it slow, head down, sort of a shuffle. He walked straight past The Smoke Shop, then flared out his long leather coat and straddled one of the high stools at the Space Station.

The Space Station was out-of-date-high-tech sci-fi. Sleek futuristic lines, metal, space-age shapes, and those cool, stark colors—black, silvers and greys. The tables were like ice-cream cones, pointed at the bottom, sliced off by cold flat surfaces where the ice cream should have been. He scanned the vegetarian menu, considering what to order. There were three drinks he especially liked. He chose the Moon Beem, a concoction of orange, papaya, banana, ginger and bee pollen, watching when the guy behind the counter got a good look at his face. The kid just nodded—okay by him—and went about his business. Minos was wondering where the kid got his big hoop earring when he heard the sound, a light snapping.

When Minos turned, there was Snapper, looking pretty much like he remembered him.

Just seeing the finger-snapping, scheming tease made Minos really mad. Snapper was nineteen now, tall, graceful, and irresistible to men and women. He carried a leather bag, like a purse, on his shoulder. He was one of those people who could get away with things, make them look easy. Dangerous things. Yeah. Because of his looks, he could fool people. Even take advantage of them. As far as Minos was concerned, Snapper was a boil on the Master's fair skin, a boil that needed lancing.

When he sat beside Minos, Snapper winked. "Hey, ugly buddy."

Minos just stared. No one could get under his skin like Snapper. He reached inside his leather coat, took out a package, set it on the counter. He watched the slut snap his fingers, check it out.

"You know, I've been thinking. El Jefe—" Snapper winked when Minos looked puzzled. "Your boss—he made a mistake. And mistakes, they are sometimes hard to fix. Even for a big cheese. You know?" Snapper tapped the package then put it in his purse. "I've been thinking what we have here is a beginning, a good beginning." He nodded once, slowly. Minos could hear his fingers snapping under the table. "See you soon. Maybe next time, you wear something, you know, not so colorful. Okay?" Another wink, and he was gone.

There it was. When Snapper left, Minos shuffled along behind him, keeping back, watching. His mind was working now too, super fast. He didn't like it when Snapper called the Master names, like boss, or El Jefe— whatever that was—or big cheese.

At the entrance to Urban Outfitters, Snapper met another boy. He was really good-looking, like the Snapper, only buff with this shoulder-length, red-orange hair. And the boy's very cool hair had these perfect wavy curls, like in a shampoo commercial. Minos knew this boy, though he couldn't remember his name, or where he'd met him. *Maybe it was in another life*, he thought to himself, then he smiled on the inside at his private joke.

The boys went south, down Broadway, past the Greek Restaurant. Minos followed from across the street, shuffling along just fast enough to keep them in sight. He was good at that, moving his feet in quick steps, head angled down to avoid any eye contact. They went past the taco place, past Seattle Central, stopping in at a new trance and techno spot that looked to him more like a man-sized video game, finally turning west on Pine then south toward the Blue City Café. At the café, the redheaded sweetie gave Snapper a hug. Snapper gave him a book from his purse, then the sweet-looking boy went inside. When Snapper turned back down Pine, Minos shuffled after the finger-snapping slut. He was going to talk to him, he decided, and fix this. The Master was always busy, and so kind, so forgiving, he couldn't take proper care of himself. He needed Minos for that. Okay, he'd make this problem go away, and then he'd have time to play. He had an idea for a new game.

◆◆◆

Corey was waiting at a Broadway coffee shop, sitting at the window, watching the street. She liked it here: liked the parade of color and style, the wild hair and clothes, the "hot" spots, the fringe. Her work often led to this odd adolescent mecca. Corey found runaways, and for homeless youth, Broadway was a place to hang.

This evening, she waited for Snapper, a runaway and a friend, who wanted to talk with her. As she waited, Corey was thinking, absentmindedly rubbing the back of her neck, taking in the street life. Corey was puzzled about her son Billy, wondering why a child as grounded and gifted as he wasn't more popular at school. What mattered to these kids? Looks? Money? In some ways, it was simpler on the streets. On the street, kids learned what counted early on.

In private school, she'd seen how the school community formed its own self-contained culture. Each school was a little different. At Olympic, the tone, the norms of this little society, were set by the "popular kids," a small clique of look-alikes—thin, attractive thoroughbreds—and they ruled. They dictated who was in, what was cool. There was this very specific status hierarchy—everything from grasshoppers to God had its proper rank—and everyone knew exactly where they stood at all times. She thought the administration was way too accepting of this set-up.

It hadn't been like this "in her day," as Billy would put it.

It was 1989 when Corey turned seventeen. Her mother died that year, and she lived alone on their boat, the *Jenny Ann*, supporting herself however she could. After school, while her girlfriends were shopping and talking about boys, Corey was canning fish. Summers, she fished in Alaska on a purse seiner. Still, she'd learned to like who she was, and not think too much about how other people saw it. Maybe it was easier then, she didn't know.

When Billy was almost thirteen she was framed by a corrupt lawyer. She spent twenty-two months at the Geiger Corrections Center, the Federal Prison in Spokane. When she got out she was sent to Abe for a psychiatric evaluation. The evaluation was a requirement to get her son back from foster care. After a rocky start, she and Abe connected. Together, they brought down that sonofabitch lawyer, Nick Season— who was running for State Attorney General—and she was vindicated. During her time in prison, though, it was that self-acceptance that got her through the unbearable times. The hardest times were at night, worrying about Billy in foster care.

She saw her friend Buzz weaving through the crowd toward the coffee shop. Buzz was African American. His head was shaved. He sagged his baggy pants under a sleeveless red T-shirt. Over his T-shirt Buzz wore his signature silver-studded, black jean vest. As he got closer, she couldn't miss the tattoos, wrist to shoulder. On Broadway, Buzz was a regular. She stood, flagging him down.

Buzz caught her wave and moved through the small tables, slinking into the seat across from her. "Yo, " he said.

"Hey." She smiled. Corey liked Buzz. He'd been on the street a long time, and he kept up with the gossip, or "buzz," hence his street name. "How you doing?" she asked.

"Excellent, is how I'm doing." He touched the back of her hand. "And yourself?"

"I'm okay. Yeah."

He looked around. She patted his arm. "Get something for yourself and tell me what's doing."

He gave her a thumbs up, knowing a free meal when it was offered.

When Buzz sat down again, there were three packaged sandwiches on his tray, and a nice grin on his face. He tilted his head toward the cashier, who was watching him like a hawk.

"Snapper's back," she said to him, after she'd paid his check.

"Snapper?" Buzz shook his head. "I don't think so. That boy's long gone. He split last summer."

"He called. He wants my help." She'd been hired to find Snapper by his mother. When she finally found him, almost fifteen months ago, she hid him until she could work it out with his abusive father. Mom paid her fee.

"You sure it was him?" Buzz tapped one of the rings on his right hand against the table.

"Un-huh. We talked on the phone."

"Must be danger, he asking you to help with it." Buzz nodded. "The Snapper can dodge a bullet."

It was true. Snapper was a natural-born scammer, an easy-going street hustler, and it often got him in trouble. "I was supposed to meet him here at five-thirty. He's half an hour late."

"You know the Snapper. He come by, ask you to go with him to Portland, say. You say when. He say now. He got something going. You say how long? He say who knows. Long as it take to score. The Snapper does his own thing in his own time."

Corey and Buzz talked for another ten minutes. Corey waited on after that. She was feeling edgy, up and down. Part of it was what Billy had said about the popular kids, especially how they made fun of Sara. Some of it was Snapper. Where was he? Snapper, she knew, was notoriously unreliable. Still, he'd made this sound important. Corey sat, brooding, for another ten minutes. Snapper never showed.

CHAPTER THREE

"Shrinks sap your strength," Sara complained to Abe. She was sitting in his cherry leather chair. "I know this already."

"I never thought of that," Abe admitted. He liked Sara. She was keenly observant and honest. What confused him was that these same qualities led her to another version of herself, a priestess, trying to channel Apollo's Oracle. "That can't be good," he added.

"Not good is right." Sara picked at a scab on the back of her wrist. She wore a long black dress, a long-sleeved black jersey, her spiked collar, and a simple silver necklace with a black damascene silver stallion hanging from the chain. The bright red streaks in her hair were bold as flashing neon. "I mean you want me to explain *everything*.

"What should I do?"

"The Beast is rising. I need more power, not less. Help me with my power."

"How?"

"I'm not sure yet." She spotted an old match, way under his desk, picked it up and tossed it in his big stone ashtray.

"Thanks," Abe said, realizing that even when Sara was thinking, she was scanning, taking in every little thing.

"Tell me more about the Beast."

"Why?" Sara looked right at him. "I mean…so far, when I try to tell you about the Beast—hard, scary things I'm sure on—you don't get it, at all, which frustrates me, makes me feel even worse, and saps my strength. So what's the point?"

Abe's brow furrowed; he understood all too well how she felt and why she felt that way. "Yes, you're right, I'm not getting it. But believe me, Sara, I'm trying—"

"And that's what I mean. It's not working. Trying isn't the same as understanding." She set the edge of her scab in his ashtray with her fingertips, slowing down, shifting gears. "Besides, it's not safe here."

Abe liked that she wasn't giving up. He wondered how he could make it safe. "Where can you talk about it?"

"In my magic circle. No where else."

"I think you could be safe here," he suggested.

"That's not right. This isn't safe for me or for you. The Beast could crush you like a bug."

Abe thought about this. "I'm not afraid of the Beast."

"Hah," she snorted. "Peirithous, the Lapith, he wasn't afraid." She leaned in, wound like a coil spring. "He invited the Centaurs to his wedding feast. They were wild beasts, half-horse, half-man. Since so many people came, the Centaurs were seated apart, in a cavern. They pushed away their sour milk, and filled their silver horns from the wine-skins. They were not used to wine. When Hippodameia, Peirithous' bride came to greet them, Eurytion, the Centaur, leaped from his stool, knocked over the table, and dragged her away by the hair. The other Centaurs joined in, raping women and boys. Peirithous and his best friend, Theseus, had to rescue Hippodameia. They cut off Eurytion's ears and nose. The bloody fight between the Centaurs and the Lapiths lasted into the night. And the great feud between them began. Peirithous should have been afraid." She sat back. "And so should you, mister. Period," she added.

Abe listened carefully, spellbound. "Who was Peirithous?" he eventually asked.

"Peirithous was king of the Lapiths. He was a brave king, but rash. He became Theseus' good friend, his honorary twin."

"Theseus, it seems, is a good friend to have."

"Yes and no. Theseus' friends often die." She nodded, a fact.

"Go on," was all he said.

"Theseus' horseman, his charioteer, they say he was murdered on the Isthmus Road. Sciron forced him to wash his feet, then kicked him off a cliff, into the sea, where he was devoured by a monstrous green turtle.

Later Theseus killed Sciron—he threw him from that same cliff, 'serving him as he served others.'"

Abe just nodded. She was so specific. In the world of the Beast, there were rules and harsh consequences. He made a decision. "Sara, I'd like to help you reach Theseus. I'd like to help you fight the Beast. Think about how I can help. I'll follow your lead."

"Mister, this isn't like dancing." She shook her head. "I guess our time is up, huh?" And frowning, she left.

◆◆◆

Not so pretty now, are you? Minos was thinking, remembering how Snapper had looked when the drug took hold and caused him to fall and crack his head on the hardwood floor, out cold. Minos smiled, working on his plan for the Snapper, as he cruised Broadway.

He had a kernel, a sprouting seed, of a big idea. He could feel it, twisting and turning in the past, working its way into the present. He had to give it time to evolve, to grow into itself. He knew that if he didn't go too fast, didn't force it, his big idea would work itself out and present itself, fully formed, in his mind. If his instincts were right—and more and more, he had pretty good ones—he sensed that this idea could touch the past, the present and the future. He'd nurture his plan for the Snapper, let it breathe until it was ready to fly.

One more thing to do, so he turned west down Pine. Yeah. Something Snapper had said. A threat, this thing about how he was protecting his interests. That was kind of funny, because Snapper wasn't ever very careful. His idea of protection was putting on a condom, afterwards. Yeah. Minos smiled at his private little joke. Still, Minos had to be sure. He'd check it out while he waited for his plan to crystalize. He'd start with the sweet-looking boy with the curly red hair. He wondered what Snapper had given him. Maybe it was nothing, one of his come-ons. Or maybe it was something, and Minos would have to go back to work. He knew where to find out.

Ten minutes later, Minos was across from the Blue City Café, waiting in a doorway. He took out a red and white pack of Marlboroughs.

Smoking was a new game, and a good drag still gave him a little hit, without fogging his mind. He even had a lighter that worked in the wind. Minos lit up, watching and thinking. If the redheaded sweetie wasn't already in the café, he'd be there sooner or later. Teenagers were like geese or salmon, always going back to the same place.

◆◆◆

The Blue City Cafe was west of Broadway, between Pike and Pine. Over the years, the cafe had taken over the entire first floor of an old Victorian house. The main floor walls were now exposed fir posts. The downstairs had become an oversized, laid-back living room, with small groupings of sofas, tables and chairs. In one corner there was a kitchen with a tall glass counter where customers could order from an eclectic menu. In a U shaped group of couches, set against the back wall, Billy, Amy, Randy and Alex were deep in conversation, sipping their lattes. Randy and Amy were seniors. Billy and Alex were juniors at Olympic, and had been classmates since Billy transferred, almost two years ago.

Amy rested her hand on Billy's thigh as they sat, side by side, on the couch. She wore jeans and a loose brown wool sweater that couldn't hide her fine figure. Short black hair framed an intense, expressive face. Her touch was gentle, and it made him feel good about himself.

"You have to admit," Randy was saying, "Sara's alright. I mean doing that Greek Oracle shit at school. That was tight. I bet Dean 'be-your-own-self" Sentor freaked out." He rose, circling the couches with his iPhone, taking pictures. Like a restless child, Randy was always on the move.

"I heard she carved a magic circle in the bathroom floor," Amy added. "Probably made Sentor's eye start twitching." With her free hand, Amy ran her fingers through her short black hair. Her lips were full and her eyes were almost as dark as her hair. When she was listening carefully to someone, Amy pursed her lips and squinted ever so slightly, until her expression was almost feline. To Billy, everything about her was sexy.

They laughed, picturing their dean, nonplussed, eyelid working, his face covered with red blotches. During this, Randy started taking impromptu pictures with his phone. They were used to this; Randy was always taking pictures. First Billy, then Amy. Eventually, Billy and Amy posed together, arms around each other, cheek to cheek, and finally, to stop him, tongues out.

"Nice," Randy quipped. He handed the phone to Billy. "Do me and Alex."

He stood behind his boyfriend, hands on his shoulders. Randy's long, fiery red hair belonged on some Viking warrior. He was well-built, freckle-faced with handsome, delicate features. Randy whispered something in Alex's ear, then he put his hand down his shirt.

One of the popular kids, Dave, came by. "Yo sweeties, where's your voodoo bitch friend, the fire starter?" he snidely asked. "We're wondering—is she some kind of witch?"

Randy, Alex, and the others ignored him; they were used to this. Dave snorted then moved on.

After Billy took several pictures of Randy and Alex, Amy took the phone from Billy, took his picture. "I want that one," she said, taking Billy's hand.

Billy sat back down beside her, pleased she wanted his picture, unsure why she seemed to like him so much.

"What was Sara doing, anyway?" Alex asked, after a moment. Blond, blue-eyed Alex was from stern, Scandinavian stock, and he was often teased for being so serious. His sea-blue eyes took in everything, and he thought about what to say before he said it. When he spoke, he spoke softly, and his friends listened carefully.

"She told me she's afraid that her friends are in danger." Randy shrugged, raised his hands. His expression, however, was serious. "She was worried about The Horseman and Peirithous, whoever they are. Sara said she's trying to raise Theseus. She says that's why she's calling up the Oracle or whatever the hell it is she's doing," Randy explained, frowning now. He was up again, moving around, snapping more pictures of other people in the café.

When he took a picture at a table with popular seniors, Dave raised his middle finger. Randy blew Dave a kiss.

Minos waited, preoccupied. He was thinking about the Snapper, about how he thought he was so cool, so good-looking. About how he made fun of the Master. Minos was picturing him now, waking up—strapped to the gurney, his mouth taped shut. In his mind, he could see the fear in Snapper's eyes.

It came to him then—clear as a bell—his plan for the Snapper. It just popped. And now, Minos could see it—crystal clear—in his head. A death mask to send the Snapper to the underworld. The Cretan Bull, a likeness. He pictured the Cretan Bull then, trapped in the underworld. Tormented by the furies in Tartarus, a prison of eternal suffering. He felt a chill, a frisson. Yes, it was just right. Perfect. Even poetic.

Yes, the Master would be pleased and proud.

♦♦♦

Randy went from table to table, snapping pictures. It never occurred to Randy that he might be intrusive; he simply marched to the beat of his own devil-may-care drum. At times, Randy was reckless, or had an attitude; and often, he was not quite as prepared, or as smart, as he needed to be. They all remembered when Randy had hitchhiked to LA on a whim and run out of money. No problem. He sold uppers to an undercover cop to pay his way back. "Sara thinks she's protecting us," Randy added, an afterthought.

"Weird. From what? What kind of danger?" Billy asked. Something about this made him uneasy.

"She says there's this beast—yeah, that's what she calls it—anyway this beast kills people. He's rising—I think that's like waking up. She thinks he's going to kill again."

"How could she know that?" Amy wondered.

Randy shrugged. "She says she just knows."

"That's pretty crazy," Alex weighed in softly.

"This is getting too serious," Randy interrupted. "Sara's just Sara. Since she was little she had her own made-up ideas about things. There's nothing we can do about the way she is. She's pretty much in her own zone." He shrugged again, scratching his head through long red curls. "When Peter gets back, it'll be better. He's the only one who understands what she's talking about." And, they all knew, the one who'd most often kept Randy out of trouble. When Randy would casually tempt fate, as if that was no big thing, Peter was usually there to bail him out. Since he left, Alex had stepped up, but so far, he didn't have Peter's flair for great escapes.

"When's Peter coming back anyway?" Billy asked. He'd met Peter and heard stories about him, but he didn't really know him.

"He doesn't really have a plan. You know what he's like. Sara says she got a postcard from Amsterdam. That he'll be back this summer."

"How long has he been gone?"

"Ten months, more or less. He left last summer. He's got the whole year before college. When he's ready, he'll be back. Anyway, he's the only one who can make sense of her stuff."

That didn't seem quite right to Billy, but he let it go. "It's Thursday. I've got a ton of homework," was all he said.

"Me too," Amy added. "Come to my place and we can work."

Billy put his arm around her slender waist as they rose to leave. She was as tall as he was.

Randy reached in his backpack, took out a book and handed it to Amy. "For the architecture project," he said.

Billy noticed that Dave was watching Amy.

"Thanks," she stuffed it in her pack. When she saw Dave staring at her, she rested her hand on Billy's backside.

Outside, Billy saw a man hunched over in a doorway across the street. The man was dressed entirely in black, and he seemed to be shuffling back and forth, staring at the sidewalk. He was on something, or just weirded out, Billy thought. Something about the way he was moving back and forth—you couldn't really tell how old he was. Billy kept his eye on him, liking his long leather coat. He watched the man light a cigarette— inhaling deeply, deliberately, like it was a special treat, then blowing the smoke into the air. That's when the man glanced up, for just an instant, and Billy saw the purple birthmark on his face. The man's left eye twisted shut when he smiled.

Billy thought he was smiling at him.

❖❖❖

At the corner of Nineteenth and Galer, on Capitol Hill, five streets came together in what Sara thought of as the "Italian intersection." The southern tip of Interlaken Park, just a finger, reached up to close the northern edge of the circle. It was below Volunteer Park, a straight shot down Galer from the cemetary where Bruce Lee was buried. Sara sort of smiled, remembering that, as she carried her things down Interlaken, the street that wound into the park. Before long she was passing the Hebrew Academy, a lonely little outpost on the hillside, then turning down again into the wooded area. Her spot was more than a hundred yards from the road, hidden in a small stand of firs. She scrambled down the hill, out of sight. She knew just where she was going. This time of year, there was never anyone down there during the day. At night, there were some drug dealers, or so she'd heard, but she'd never seen them. Surrounded by her trees, Sara began unpacking her bags. In addition to her canvas shoulder bag, Sara had a black duffle bag filled with the heavier things she needed to reach the Oracle.

After chanting over the salt and the water, then sprinkling the mixture around her magic circle, making it safe, Sara set the little iron cauldron on her tripod. She double-checked, making sure it sat right in the center of the large circle.

Today, she said an extra blessing as she made the sign of the cross on her forehead. She was careful to keep her first and second fingers extended, and the third and fourth bent toward her palm with the thumb on their nails. She'd recently read in a book on psychic defense that that was the way to do it. Satisfied, she continued unpacking her bags. From her canvas shoulder bag she took olive oil, wine, and milk, pouring a splash of each into the cauldron. Beneath the cauldron she lit a propane fire, then she added herbs, rock salt, and finally, a lock of hair. From her black tote bag, she took her candles and set them at each of the five points of the star in her circle. Sara lit the candles and said another prayer.

She raised her Athame high, chanting, "I call on the Oracle of Delphi, servant of Apollo, the lord of the silver bow." She added more wine. Sara closed her eyes, drinking wine Ambrosia now from a soft plastic bottle, moving slowly around the cauldron, which was beginning to bubble. "Hear me great Apollo, serpent-slayer. I summon your Oracle." Her movements were a little faster. Wine Ambrosia ran down her chin. "I must find Theseus. There is great danger. Help me now." Sara stared into the bubbling cauldron. Hands in the air. Watching, waiting. "Give me a sign. Hear your priestess. Secret sister of Theseus. Oh mighty Apollo, God of truth, hear me now. Poseidon has been scorned. The Beast is rising." She slowed, raised her Athame high, still staring at the boiling potion in her cauldron. She swayed back and forth, summoning the Oracle, eyes on the boiling potion. And louder, "Nothing. You grant me nothing. Then there must be blood. The gods must dance in blood." Sara stiffened, and with one fluid motion, she brought her Athame down, slicing across her forearm. "Accept my offering, great Apollo, keeper of light. And to you, Poseidon, earth-shaker, I offer again to you, to appease your anger." Sara sliced again, letting her blood flow down her elbow and into the bubbling cauldron. "Hear me. Hear me now. Bring me Theseus. Show me his sign." She raised her arm again, watching the blood swirling in her potion. In the cooling shadows of the spring afternoon, Sara raised her Athame high and danced lightly around her simmering cauldron.

CHAPTER FOUR

On Tuesday morning, Sara saw Abe at 10:00. This was her second Tuesday, and as far as she was concerned, they were stuck. He wasn't mean or anything; he just got in the way, took up valuable time. And now—time was running out, so every minute counted. She only had time at all, she was painfully aware, because she'd been suspended. Which wasn't about to end, even when people started dying.

And that got her going again, about her school. At Olympic, when you were suspended, you were toast. They didn't want to see you. Period.

And home schooling was like some cruel joke. Sara had given up on the freeze-dried lady whose sphincter tightened right up—she was sure on this—every time Sara tugged at her nose ring. She raised her black sweater to her elbow, checking her bandage. One of her cuts had been deeper than she'd realized, and it wasn't healing. Mostly, she didn't want it to start bleeding again. Sara was checking out the waiting room, wondering what to tell her dad if he noticed her bandages—and he probably would, he was almost as observant as she was—when Dr. Stein, the bear-shrink, opened his office door.

It didn't matter how many times he changed his sport coat, he always looked rumply. His salt and pepper hair was perpetually like totally tousled. His beard, even when he trimmed it, was uneven. His office always had this messy, smoker feel—she could smell his Butternut Burley pipe tobacco from the waiting room—even when it was clean and aired out. And this guy wanted to help her. How could he fight the Beast if he couldn't even comb his own hair? Huh? It made her mad, like he didn't take her seriously or something. She was getting tired of this. Yeah, she was awfully tired and so out of time.

Inside, they started out as usual. She just sat there, and he waited. She figured this waiting business burned up maybe three, four minutes every fifty-minute hour.

This time, he didn't wait; he didn't even bother to fire up the blackened bowl of his stinky pipe. "Sara, there's no point in working together if I can't help you. So far, I don't think I'm helping."

"Right." Sara nodded agreement. "So far, you're not helping. You're hurting." She watched him take this in.

Abe leaned in. Sara liked how all the wrinkly lines in his face turned down when he was really trying. "How am I hurting?" he asked.

"I already explained this. You don't hear me, or, if you do, you don't believe what I say."

"I do believe you, Sara, always, even when I don't understand. You can count on that. Please, let's try again."

Sara thought about this. She wished she knew a different way to talk about it. She didn't. It came out the way it was; she could only say what she knew. She'd try her best, too, but she didn't think it would work. He didn't have a way to think about what she said. "Do you understand Moira?"

"A little…but I'd like to know more."

"It's your fate. It's stronger even than the gods. If you scorn Moira, you absolutely bring Nemesis." Sara saw she was going too fast. "That's righteous anger. Very bad news." She nodded, sure on this. "When you recognize it—Moira, that is—you just know what to do."

He considered this. "And do you know your Moira?"

"Yeah. Definitely. Fight the Beast. I have to stop him. It's time. He's rising. He's going to kill soon, if he hasn't killed already. Like Phaea, the monstrous wild white sow, he knows no mercy. Like Cerberus, the three-headed, dragon-tailed dog who guards the gates of Hell, who permits all spirits to enter but none to leave; he isn't what he seems. The Horseman is coming. I have to find him…warn him. The Beast is rising—"

"Who's the Horseman?" Abe asked.

"Theseus' charioteer." Sara took a breath, continuing. "The Beast is rising. And no one hears me. No one is even listening."

"I'm listening."

She shook her head, no. "The sow killed so may Crommyonians that they dared not plough their fields. Theseus hunted down that wild beast and killed it. He didn't talk about it. It wasn't a game. When he sailed to Crete, to face the Minotaur, it wasn't a game. He knew he had to slay a vicious child-eating monster. Whenever the great earth-shaker, Poseidon, gave Theseus a sign, he listened. I need his help. But he doesn't hear me. I can't reach him, no matter how hard I try. Has some god struck Theseus deaf? Why are they angry? What has happened? Poseidon isn't listening. Apollo isn't listening. Zeus, the all-knowing, he isn't even listening."

"I'm listening," Abe repeated.

"You're not hearing."

"Go on."

"I need the Gods, I need Poseidon, and Apollo. I need Theseus to fight the Beast. It's not a trick. It's not a game. I'm not crazy. When I told them at school, they made me see you. They thought I was mental, you know, troubled. When Cassandra failed to pay Apollo for the gift of prophecy, he spit in her mouth, and thereafter, no one believed her. Has Apollo, the truth sayer, spit in my mouth as well? No one even listens to me. The Beast is rising, and he's going to kill. He's going to kill my friends. Can you hear that? He may have killed already."

"How do you know?"

She stood, pressing the toe of her black boot into the carpet. "You don't have to watch Poseidon's wild, white bull mount Daedalus' wooden cow with Pasiphae hidden inside—lusting for this bestial act—to know that he sired the Minotaur." Sara looked up at him, defiant. "Can you imagine that? Can you understand it?" she eventually asked. He was studying her, she could tell, even when she stared back down at the floor. Maybe that was how he thought about things. Maybe he thought if he studied her long enough, he could get inside her mind or something.

"No, I don't really understand," he finally admitted. And then, after a moment, "Sara, could we try another way? Could we talk about your friends...or your family?... If I could learn more about those things, I might have an easier time understanding how to help you find Theseus..."

Sara closed her eyes and started chanting. What was he thinking? What was he doing? She felt a stirring. Shit. She had to do something. It was bad enough when it happened at school. Why was this happening here? Not today. Unh-un. Without another word, Sara turned and left.

Abe rose, then sat down again, watching her go.

♦♦♦

Whenever she walked Broadway, Corey felt old. She knew every shop and every stoop. Still, Broadway was as mysterious to her as the mountains on the moon.

At the near corner, there was a Diamond parking lot, bordered by a low wall. On some days, the wall was a place to hang for some of the street kids she knew. Today, she stopped to ask Cash—a fifteen-year-old girl who worked the streets, "spanging" for lose change—about Snapper. Cash was high on something, but willing to talk. Sure, she'd known him. No, he wasn't back. California, maybe. Yeah, that was it. No one else on the wall knew anything or wanted to know anything. It made her a little antsy, a feeling she hadn't been able to shake since Snapper didn't show at Starbucks. And she was anxious, though she didn't know why.

Further south, Corey stopped at the little round window of a hole-in-the-wall Greek restaurant. Inside, she could see Johnny Boy, a skinny, fair, confident young man with short brown hair. When she'd first met him, he was hustling older men on the street. She'd helped his "street sister" get away from her pimp, and they became friends. With a little encouragement, he started selling *Real Change*, a paper largely written and sold by the homeless. Later, he became a dishwasher at a Thai restaurant. Now, he was a waiter, almost a headwaiter to hear him tell it, at this tiny Greek deli. He was twenty and Johnny Boy was getting married in July. JB waved when he saw her. Before she even sat down, he had placed a bowl of the spicy black olives she liked in front of her.

"Taking a break," he called out as he sat opposite her at one of the four small tables. Most of the long narrow room was given over to a large display case. Carefully presented inside the case were salads, cold cuts, and Greek specialties like grape leaves, gyros, or baklava. She took a moment to admire the display. Corey knew this was Johnny Boy's responsibility, and he was rightly proud of it.

Corey ordered a cup of the strong Greek coffee. "Nervous?" she asked.

"Whenever I think about it."

"How's Tiffany?"

"Better than me. Her mom came all the way from Georgia to help her pick out her wedding dress. She hasn't seen her mom in six years."

"Nice."

"I dunno. You have to picture this. Her mom, Martha, she cleans people's houses; she goes to church twice every day; every Sunday, she helps with the Baptisms. Now Tiff takes her shopping on Broadway, to the Ave. I mean everywhere. At Retro Viva, this sales girl has the Dark Prince tattooed on her arm, and she's fully loaded—studs everywhere, rings in her nose, her navel, this chain is hooked from her ear to her lip. So Martha blesses her, then she makes the sign of the cross with her fingers, and backs out of the store."

Corey smiled. "I need some help."

"Shoot."

"Remember Snapper?"

"A little more than a year back?" JB bit his thumbnail as he put it together. "The smart-ass kid I hid in my squat? His old man wanted to bust him up."

"Yeah. What do you know about him?"

"He hooked up with another guy. I think it was pretty serious. Snapper had some money, and I heard they split to California somewhere. I haven't seen him in—I dunno—a year."

"You know the boyfriend?"

"Un-unh. Once you cooled out the dad, Snapper left the rat hole I had him living in. I saw him around, after, but I never met his guy."

"He's back. Snapper called me. Set a meeting then didn't show up. I need to find him. Can you ask around?"

"Sure. I remember one of his friends. I'll talk with him."

"See what you can find out about the boyfriend, too."

"You got it," Johnny Boy said. "Uh-huh."

"How about I take out dinner?"

"I'll put it together. Lemme see." He looked over the display, tapping the window, mumbling to himself. JB turned to her, serious. "Can I ask you for something, a really big favor?"

"Sure."

"Please say no if you don't want to do it."

"Of course."

Corey watched him, taking a breath, screwing up his courage. "OK... here goes..." Another breath. "Would you be in my wedding, walk me down the aisle?"

Corey smiled wide as tears came to her eyes. "I'd love to do that."

"You're the only one I could think of that I really wanted to do it. So...so thank you."

Corey stood, taking his hands.

◆◆◆

Abe hadn't moved much since Sara left. He was confused, floundering, and he wasn't sure what to do. Much of his early work had been with felons. At one time, almost half of his practice came through post-prison programs. And often, he hadn't known what to believe, what was real. He'd learned little things to listen for, what to ask, and he'd come to trust his impressions and his judgment. Once he ferreted out what was real, finding common ground and setting goals, even unconventional goals, became possible.

Sometimes, and Corey was the best example of this, everything his client was saying was true. At those times, his work was simply to get that. It always took too long. In Corey's case, before he understood what was at stake, she and Billy were gone, running for their lives. He'd found her, worked it out. It changed his life forever, especially the way he thought, the way he saw things.

Since meeting Corey, Abe's practice had changed, too. Though he kept his office in the dusty brick building under the viaduct with the fragrant Chinese restaurant on the first floor, he now spent most of his time working with troubled kids and their families, offering a practical combination of medication and therapy. Sorting out a child's reality could be even more complicated than working with felons. Often, a troubled child believed something to be true in spite of overwhelming evidence to the contrary. Usually, it was part of some larger belief system, perceived to be held by a trusted or an intimidating authority. For example he'd known a child to insist that their euthanized pet was on a farm, because the parents had told that lie.

In Sara's case, he was certain she wasn't lying. She believed what she said. He also thought that she'd created this entire complex universe—even developed her own language—by herself. No one—not her father, her teachers, nor her friends—was encouraging her to look to the Greek gods for a mortal hero, protection and guidance. And, he was sure, she'd fashioned that magical world in response to something. Yes, he sensed that she was trying, desperately, to communicate some terrible, otherwise inaccessible knowledge. It wasn't something she could tell him—or she wouldn't have created her world in the first place. No, he'd have to learn her language.

His size thirteen feet, in ancient Italian brown leather shoes, were propped on his desk, and he faced the cherry leather chair that she'd been sitting in. It was close, kitty-corner from his own chair, a straight shot across the corner of his table-sized desk. He could still see her sitting there, taking in every nuance, as she carefully explained how the Beast would kill soon. A simple fact, plain as the nose on his face.

He was taking a risk; he knew that. The conventional thing would be to medicate her, then, if necessary, have her hospitalized. But Abe knew he'd never be able to help her if he did that. Someone had to hang in with her, learn to speak her magical, made-up language. And figure out with her what she actually meant by it. Who was Theseus? Why did she need him? Who was the Beast? Why was he so dangerous? She was getting at something that was, he thought, too frightening for consciousness. And in spite of that, she was trying to warn him. Why did he believe her? He didn't know. Hell, he admired her. That was the truth.

And he didn't know what to do. He didn't think that she'd hurt herself—though the gods in her carefully crafted, universe could be dangerously punitive. She certainly wasn't a threat to anyone else. And so far as he knew, no one had been hurt yet. He thought about her warning. He couldn't see who, if anyone, was about to die. That was still vague. Harsh punishments, often death, were real consequences in her mythological universe. And her worry about someone dying could easily come from some past injustice, too frightful to bear. He shook his head—no—a gesture, he realized, he'd picked up from Sara. He was rationalizing, and he knew it. He didn't know what she was getting at, and he didn't know what to do about that, or even where to turn. She had no interest in talking about anything in the present—school, family, friends. No time for it. In fact, it made her mad. She rolled her eyes and started chanting whenever he asked a question about those things. Or she'd ignore his question and race back into the past.

And she was right—he was hurting, not helping, that is to say slowing her down, wasting her valuable energy. She was explaining things to him, over and over, and even after her explanations, he plainly didn't understand. Okay, this was a problem he had to engage, even if he couldn't solve it. He stared at his cherry leather chair, confounded.

He'd see her again tomorrow. Maybe there was a way to talk about Theseus. Abe wanted to pick up a book on Greek mythology, see what he could learn about Theseus, the king. At least he'd see if he could listen to her in a way that was helpful. He stood, frowning, still perplexed, as he gathered his things, putting them in his worn, brown-leather briefcase. He was off to talk with Owen Sentor, Olympic's high school counselor and acting dean, to see what he wasn't listening to.

◆◆◆

After any given school day, the table against the far wall at the Blue City Café was the first stop for Billy and his friends. Today, Randy, Alex, and Amy were hanging out, waiting for Billy to come from an after school spring soccer meeting. Randy was showing off the pictures he'd taken, then printed from his computer. When he saw that his friends were only interested in how they looked, he stashed them in his backpack.

Randy saw her first and waved her over. Sara was dressed in black, walking very slowly, talking to herself. She carried her bulging canvas shoulder bag. Sara fingered a spike on her collar as she made her way to their table.

"Hey, Sara," Randy greeted her as she sat down. "What's up?"

She sat, shook her head. "There's danger. I'm scared. The Beast is going to kill again. I need to raise Theseus." Matter of fact.

Randy nodded. They were used to this. "Hey, I thought it was pretty cool, the way you tried to reach the Oracle at school. You know, that business in the bathroom."

"It didn't work," she said, resigned. "And now I'm suspended."

"Sentor means well. He's just not up to something like this."

"He's a dick, a total zero. I laid a pretty heavy curse on him."

Randy and Alex slapped palms, a high five, liking that.

"They'll let you back," Alex said.

"I dunno. I have to get professional help, you know? A shrink. It's not working out too well."

"Sorry," Amy volunteered. "I can't see how a shrink would understand your stuff. I mean it's hard for us to understand."

Sara's thin face turned sad, weary. "Tell me about it."

"Does your brother still get it?" Alex asked.

Sara almost smiled. Just thinking about Peter picked her up. "Yeah, he would. But Peter's in Europe."

Russ and Dave came by their table. Dave leaned in toward Sara, "Yo, voodoo bitch," he said, then he winked at her. "Can you lift the dreaded curse off of Amy here," He smirked, pointed a forefinger at Amy. "Lift that chastity curse so that one day 'the vice' can spread her legs."

Amy looked up, squinted. "When we want your shit, we'll squeeze your head."

Alex and Randy exchanged high fives, again, as Russ and Dave stalked off.

"Thanks," Sara said, then pointed at Amy's drink. "Mocha?"

"How'd you know?"

"Mocha has its own smell." She sniffed, nodded. "Can I have some?"

"Uh-huh. Sure."

Amy passed her cup as Randy asked, "Have you heard from Peter?"

For the first time, Sara cracked a trace of a smile. "My dad did, at the clinic. He called from London. No kidding. Peter's going to the Greek islands. It's like a dream come true. He said he'll be back in July. He's going to call or write from Crete."

"That's Peter. You know he's on a terrific boat too," Randy said. "The guy's got the touch."

"It's called charisma," Alex corrected his boy friend. At times, Sara thought Alex was jealous of Randy. Even though he knew there was no good reason—for godsake, Peter was his friend, too. Still, Peter had been Randy's best friend forever. They'd always been good together. Peter's keen, practical intelligence gently tempered Randy's wild exuberance, his daring. And they shared a passion for exploring, taking the road not taken. Alex was more cautious, expressing his own intensity in other ways. "Peter makes his own luck," Alex explained, ruefully.

They all agreed. Peter did that. And he was missed.

Sara was about to go on when she saw Billy heading for their table. She looked away.

Billy sat on the couch, next to Amy, who put her hand behind his neck and kissed him. Billy made Sara uncomfortable. She knew why, too.

"Hey Sara." Billy smiled at her.

She looked down at the table, mumbling something. She was thinking about telling them who her shrink was. These kids were nice to her, the only ones. But Billy made it too complicated. She couldn't say what she felt right now anyway—that his dad was lame.

She felt Randy's hand on her shoulder. "You okay?" he asked.

She was mumbling, talking to herself. "Apollo, serpent slayer, keeper of the light…" Sara stood, waved a little wave, and walked away, still mumbling.

"What's with her?" Billy asked.

"It's getting worse," Randy said. "I'm going to talk with her dad, see if we can help."

Amy pulled Billy over. Kissed him again. "I missed you," she whispered, between kisses.

♦♦♦

Minos was at his special, secret place—his lab. He'd built the lab in a small out-of-the-way guesthouse on Capital Hill. It was off the street, overlooking a steep ravine. The guesthouse cantilevered over the edge of the ravine. The big picture window at the back faced north toward Lake Washington. From his worktable, he could see the lake beyond the steep drop off.

His Skytron Halogens were on, and Minos was at his makeup table, working on Snapper. On the work table he had his makeup supplies: an assortment of RMG color wheels, brushes, sponges, setting powder, liquid latex for scars, translucent face powder, cold cream, spirit gum, spirit gum remover, rubbing alcohol, and pretty much anything else a makeup artist might ever need.

"The Snapper" was on his back, strapped onto a stretcher, breathing slowly, alive but anesthetized. Carefully, Minos fitted the foam latex prosthetic makeup appliance, a mask made from foam that is injected into a mold, to Snapper's face. He admired the mask. He'd been working on it every spare minute, which, he knew, pleased the Master. He'd just applied spirit gum and the appliance was sticking nicely. When he had it just so, Minos took out a photo, the same photo he'd referenced when he made the mold. The picture showed an older man, his face battered and badly scarred from years of boxing. There were also fresh cuts and bruises from a recent fight. Minos began carefully applying makeup to the well-crafted appliance, detailing the cuts, bruises and scars to look precisely like the scarred boxer in the photo.

Sometime later, when he was ready to take a break from this careful and deliberate work, Minos sat back, looking closely at the photo, then stared out the window toward the lake.

He was thinking about the man in the photo, his father. His "babaka" was an immigrant from Crete, a tough, uneducated, though highly intelligent, man who worked repairing commercial fishing boats at

Seattle's Fisherman's Terminal. In Crete, he'd been a fisherman by trade, but first and foremost, he was a boxer, known as the Cretan Bull. In Seattle, amateur boxing had become his hobby, and his passion, and he took his son to watch him fight. In the ring, the Cretan Bull was known for his ruthless, unrelenting attacks, and his ability to withstand brutal punishment. Pacific Northwest Amateur Boxing Association aficionados praised him as a brilliant tactician. At thirty-five, he won the heavyweight division of the Seattle Golden Gloves. As a child, his son had sat in his corner during his fights, watching the Cretan Bull's trainer tend to his cuts—brow, nose, lips, and face.

His father had tried to teach him to box, but young Minos hadn't liked it.

He thought then of Minos, the Bull King, whose father was Zeus, the most powerful of all of the gods.

◆◆◆

"Thanks, Owen, for finding this time for me," Abe said, as he sunk into the dean's corduroy couch. The kids liked Owen's cluttered office. Books were piled high. The walls were covered with funny old condom posters, cult movie one-sheets—*Reefer Madness* prominent among them. He had no desk, just an antique maple table in the center of the room, for people to gather around. His office felt old, professorial. It was especially unusual at Olympic, where the tone was contemporary, clean and abstract.

"How can I help?" Owen asked, sincerely, facing Abe from his chair behind the table. Owen dressed casually, but he liked to look good. He was short and swarthy, with a neatly trimmed gray beard and a matt of gray hair on his chest. Today he wore a green and black plaid vyella shirt, fir-green, wide-corded pants, old, black-leather loafers with tassels, and an unusual woven belt with a handcrafted wooden buckle. It had some kind of tribal symbol on it.

"I need some background on Sara Peterson," Abe said, distracted. He was wondering where Owen had found that belt.

"I'm glad you're seeing her. You were on the short list I talked about with Jim."

Abe took a pipe from his pocket.

"Sorry, but my office is smoke-free," Owen explained.

Abe took out a pipe tool. "I was hoping to clean it while we talked, if that's okay."

"Sorry. No problem." Owen smiled. "I'm a little jumpy on the smoking subject." He raised his eyebrows. "You know that drill." Owen adjusted his belt, drawing attention to the engraved buckle.

"Nice." Abe pointed his pipe at the belt, nodding. He pulled over a wastebasket, went to work on his pipe. "What can you tell me about Sara?"

"Sara, Sara, Sara…she's super bright, though she's never fit in."

"Why?"

"Her own choice, I think. She's a sophomore, so she hasn't been here long. Most of that time, she's hung out with her older brother's friends and never made much of an effort with her peers."

"How old's her brother?"

"He's her half-brother, actually. I think Peter's nineteen. He graduated last year. He's on his way to Wesleyan. They gave him a year off before starting at college," Owen explained. "I encouraged him to take the year. Peter's been traveling."

"I see." Abe worked on his pipe, pensive. "How does Sara get along with her dad?"

"Pretty well, from what little I know. Jim's been in to talk about Sara several times. Our conversations have been open and, I hope, helpful. Jim's been worried about her since the fall. These past few weeks it's gotten worse."

"How so?"

"The fire in the bathroom was the last in a series of problems. Last fall, Sara asked the head of the history department, Greg Nobler, to help her research the Delphic Oracle. Greg teaches ancient Greece, and he was happy to put together a reading list for her. Then, maybe a month ago, Sara told him she needed his help again. When he asked how, she said that now, she needed to reach the Delphic Oracle. She had to find Theseus. That Apollo and Poseidon would help. She hoped he'd help her too. She's a stickler for detail, and she wanted specifics about Delphi, the priestesses, the rituals, and of course, the prophecies. He put her off. About the third time she braced him, Greg sent her to me. That first meeting, she started chanting, here in my office. She said that what she calls the 'Beast' is waking up. When I asked about it, she explained that the Beast had risen and there was danger. She couldn't specify the danger, though, then or in subsequent conversations. I recommended treatment. She wasn't interested. We met again, and I laid out the ground rules. Basically, if she wanted to stay in school, she'd have to leave her made-up mythological world at the door. She said that it would be hard to do that, and she had to think about it. At the third meeting, her dad came in with her, and she agreed to find Theseus on her own time. But she couldn't stick with our plan."

Abe kept busy with his pipe, wondering why Owen was irritating him. It was, perhaps, because Owen didn't see how acutely sensitive Sara was. And the belt. "Do you have any idea what she's referring to when she talks about the Beast?"

"That's your department, doctor. She's had more than her share of trouble, though. I know that much."

"Such as?"

"Her mother died when she was five or six." Owen checked the file. "Yes…they were on vacation in Greece when they discovered the cancer. They flew her to a hospital in London where she died. Sara was six."

Abe worked on his pipe, pensive, using his tool to scrape blackened tobacco from the bowl. He shifted gears. "I'd like to see Sara back at school, at least part-time. She needs to stay connected to what she knows."

"I take your point. Still, she's too disruptive." Owen hesitated. "Are you medicating her?"

"You know better than asking, Owen."

"Abe, that's not fair. I have to make a recommendation to a committee of faculty and administration before Sara can be readmitted. Whether or not she's taking medication to stabilize her moods is certainly a factor in my recommendation."

"I see." Abe put his pipe back in his jacket, held his tongue. "Can she come back part time?"

"Let's revisit that in a week's time. Okay?"

Abe thought this over. "I'll call you in three days. In the meantime, think about it. She needs the continuity." He stood, his brow furrowed. Owen's belt was from some country he couldn't even find on a map, like Micronesia, or Djabouti, Abe was sure of it. He turned to the dean. "Owen, what if she's right? What if she and her friends are in danger?"

"That doesn't seem very likely, does it, Abe?"

"I don't know." And he didn't. But Sara was smarter than Owen, and he'd listen to her first, any day. "Until I do, take extra care."

"Don't overreact here, okay? There's no evidence. None. Teenagers are always imagining things. I know that much."

"I don't think I'm overreacting," Abe said, as he shook Owen's offered hand.

◆◆◆

"What's duck liver rillette?" Billy wanted to know.

Corey explained that it was a coarser version of pâté, a dish he was learning to like.

At least one night a week, the Logan-Steins ate out. On one of their first evenings together, Abe had taken Corey to Chez Henri, a French restaurant at the market. She'd never been any place like it and was appalled to learn they didn't even *have* ketchup. She'd loved French food, though, and they'd been going to French restaurants ever since. Billy started joining them when he was fifteen. This Thursday evening, they were at Le Pichet, a small, authentic French Bistro on First. It was dark, lively, and smelled like garlic.

"Is it fattening?" Billy persisted.

"The worst," Abe explained, looking sadly at his stomach.

"Good," Billy said.

"Try it," Corey suggested, knowing Billy was trying to bulk up. She barely managed a smile, still worried about Snapper. Corey decided to try talking to clear her head. "Remember Snapper?" she asked.

"The good-looking kid you kept at the house one night?" Abe was sipping single malt scotch.

"That's the one. Wild, but good-hearted."

"What I remember is how he ate everything in the fridge," Billy said. "And I think he came on to me, but I was still fifteen, so I can't say for sure."

"You never told me that."

"You think I tell you all the guys who come on to me?"

A waitress with a thick French accent interrupted to take their orders. "Bien," she said when Billy asked for the rillette.

"Are there a lot of guys hitting on you?" Corey asked, vaguely irritated at this idea.

Billy sighed. "Where do we live, mom? What neighborhood?"

"Capitol Hill?"

"And?"

"It has the highest percentage of registered Democratic voters in the country," Abe volunteered.

"Okay. I know it has a significant gay community," Corey admitted. "But who else comes on to you?"

"I'm not gay, Mom. But at Olympic, some of my friends are gay, like Randy and Alex. And their friends sometimes come on to me at parties, you know."

"Olympic is its own weird little world isn't it?"

"It's worked out pretty well," Abe suggested.

"Sorry," Corey offered. "Tell me more about Olympic."

"It can be a weird place. You're not wrong about that," Billy acknowledged. "I mean I like my friends, and Amy's the best. But we're so far out of the mainstream."

"Why?"

"There's no choice. It's like if you don't fit in—if you're fat or different or ugly or simply not willing to play the game—you're exiled. For the popular kids at Olympic, I'm like this total loser. I mean I'm not even on their radar screen. There are all kinds of parties that I'm not invited to. Dances and things we just don't go to because we don't feel part of things." As he explained, Billy watched his stepdad. Corey knew Billy liked the way Abe soaked it all up, like this great big sponge. "Those of us who don't care," he specified. "We're stone dead." Billy raised his eyebrows, his palms. "Outcasts…"

"What kind of school lets that happen?" Corey wanted to know, irritated now. She felt Abe's big hand on her shoulder. She answered the question herself. "The same school that didn't believe me when I said last year that Maisie and Aaron were in danger."

"And now they're not listening to Sara." Billy was busy, eating his rillette. He looked up. "What if she's right?" he wanted to know. "What if we're all in danger?"

Corey turned to Abe. "Let's *assume* she's right. What can we do…Abe?"

Abe was quiet.

"Why are you asking dad?"

"He's working with her."

"What?"

Abe was scowling. "That's confidential."

"Owen told Amber—he wanted her opinion about whether you'd helped Maisie. Amber told me, so I figure the word's out."

"Owen's out of line." Abe's long, lined face showed just how he felt about that.

"So straighten him out, but if Amber can tell me how happy she is that you're helping Sara, I can tell Billy. Right?"

"Yes, though I'll have to explain all of this to Sara."

Billy was scowling now, like his dad. "Well that explains why she's so unfriendly."

"I'll tell her you know, then you can work it out with her. Sorry to put you in an awkward situation."

Billy touched his dad's arm, an affectionate gesture. "A mom who's sure about everything. A dad who knows more about my friends than I do…" He shrugged. "That's my life…" He shrugged again.

Corey smiled, proud of her son. "Yeah that pretty much sums it up… so what if Sara's right? What if Billy and his friends are in danger?"

"It's up to you to figure it out, isn't it?" Billy asked his stepfather.

Abe didn't say anything.

"Yes." Corey pursed her lips.

◆◆◆

The redhead had it all: great looking, rich, no one looking over his shoulder. Lucky, is what he was. He even lived in this great big old wooden house, right across from Volunteer Park. Perfect. Lucky Red could cruise the park for pick-ups while his dad had his cocktail on the huge front porch. The mom didn't live there. He already knew that. Which made it easier. Fathers never really knew about their sons. Un-unh. Never knew what they were doing or thinking. His dad didn't even care what he thought, so long as Minos did what he was told. No, his dad was strict, old-fashioned in the Cretan way. One time, when he was late, his father whipped him with his belt, then locked him in the basement for two days. It made Minos mad, thinking about it; so he stopped, before he got a headache.

Minos was in the bushes across from the big house when Lucky Red came out again. Only this time he didn't have his backpack. Where had he seen him before, he wondered. Did the Master know him? Sometimes, he didn't recognize the Master's friends, people he should know. He was getting better at it, though. Little by little.

Lucky Red, was, he thought, as handsome as Ganymedes, the most beautiful youth alive, chosen by the gods to be Zeus's cupbearer. Zeus desired him and eventually, disguised in eagle feathers, Zeus abducted him and took him as his lover. Minos considered abducting Lucky Red, giving him to the Master. He could picture the Master, making love to Lucky Red. And killing him, after.

Ten minutes later Minos forced open the back door. It made his heart pump pretty fast. Going through other people's things without their knowing was one of his games. He was still working at putting things back just so. Today, though, he wasn't just playing. Today, he was taking care of the Master. Once he'd checked out what Snapper had given Lucky Red, he'd be able to play. Snapper eventually admitted that he'd given the "proof" to Lucky Red, and, under the circumstances, Minos believed him. Later, Snapper explained that he told Red to hide it, that he'd meet him in three days. In the meantime he didn't want anyone else to know that he was back. Not unless anything happened to him, that is. It occurred to Minos that starting today, maybe Lucky Red wasn't so lucky after all.

The boy's bedroom was easy to find. Less than a minute in the house and Minos was going through the backpack. Inside, he found a bunch of books. He went through the books, one by one. The buff boy's name was Randy, and he had textbooks—math, chemistry, and history—and a book about art history. Nothing special or even unusual about any of them. Huh. At the bottom of the pack, he saw the pictures—four by sixes, printed from a computer. He took them out. Randy the redhead, and his pals. This one had to be his lover boy. Minos kept it. And this one was the tall sassy kid who looked at him when he was smoking in front of the café. He didn't like that kid. Un-unh. And Minos didn't like the tall girl that was on his arm, either. In the next picture, the sassy kid and his long-legged twist were together, sticking out their tongues, like they wanted to play. He'd keep that one, too. He'd play all right. Maybe he'd teach them his new game.

◆◆◆

"And Zeus?" Abe asked. He was seated, listening to Sara. He'd stayed up late reading the sections on Theseus, Poseidon, Apollo and Zeus in Robert Grave's *The Greek Myths*. He now understood that Theseus was a hero, capable of amazing feats. He also understood that it was Apollo's Oracle at Delphi. That no other shrine rivaled it.

Sara didn't respond. It was as if she hadn't heard his question. In the silence, she grew distracted. Then her expression turned grim.

Abe was waiting, watching her. When the sun came through the blinds, he noticed her face and neck were flushed.

She wrapped her arms around herself, muttering softly.

"Can you smell the Beast?" he asked, out of nowhere.

Sara curled up, readying herself. She groaned as if something had stirred in her stomach. "No," she said, a whisper. "It's not that. Un-unh."

"What is it?" Abe asked.

"I feel something." She frowned, uncertain, uncurling with a gasp. Then, "Oh Jesus," she whispered. Her face had turned red. Little beads of sweat lined her brow. Sara swayed, back and forth, groaning softly.

"Are you okay?" Abe could see the sweat now, dripping down her face. She ignored him. The veins in her face were throbbing, pulsing blue lines. Her eyeballs rolled under her eyelids. Sara stood, slowly, carefully, whispering, "Oracle of Delphi, I anoint your stone with oil." She was in some kind of a trance. "Oh great Apollo, bearer of light. I am your priestess, the pythoness, your vestal virgin." She raised her arms. Sara's face was red and wet, veins bulging.

Sara waved her arms in the air, crying out, "Take me. I am your vessel. Let me cry out your prophecy." She was moving now, shaking her arms.

Abe leaned in.

"Oh god. Oh my god," she whispered, grasping her stomach. "Let me speak with thy voice…" Then Sara raised her arms higher still, moving faster, as if possessed. She made guttural noises, whispering unintelligible words, groaning, hissing, and then she was quiet, transfixed, eyes on some distant point out the window. When she finally spoke, her voice was frenzied. "Minos' philandering so angered his wife, Pasiphae, that she cast a spell on him: whenever he made love to another woman, he discharged no seeds. Instead, he unleashed snakes, scorpions and centipedes, which fed on her internal organs until she died."

Sara swayed, side-to-side, crying out, "…serpents…scorpions… centipedes…" Sweat fell from her brow. She called out, "Pasiphae made love to the great white bull. She gave birth to the Minotaur. She gave Minos eight children. Minos the king, keeper of her Minotaur…" her voice trailed off as she went deeper into her trance.

"What?"

She didn't hear him. Sara was crying out now, twirling, shaking her arms in the air. She was right in front of his desk when the cut on her forearm opened and blood began to run down her arm.

Abe quickly came around the desk and lowered her back into her chair. Sara kept chanting, oblivious. Abe gently raised her arm in the air, then lowered the sleeve of her sweater to reveal where her wound had opened. It was bleeding slowly but steadily. He carefully reapplied her bandage, then Abe took a roll of gauze and some surgical tape from his first aid kit. He wrapped the gauze around her bandage then taped it. He adjusted her bandage until the bleeding stopped. When he was finished, Abe knelt in front of her. "What happened?" he asked, gently.

Sara just looked at him, still in her trance. She pushed him away.

Abe thought he knew what he'd seen. He'd read how Apollo had seized the Delphic Oracle, and retained its priestess, called the Pythoness or the Pythia, in his service. The Pythia went into a trance, allowing Apollo to possess her spirit. In this state, she prophesied.

"What happened?" he asked again.

She wiped her forehead with her sleeve.

"Were you the Pythia?" he asked.

She nodded, arms around her stomach again.

"Here?"

Sara fingered a spike on her collar. "Apollo was possessing my spirit, warning me about Pasiphae...and Minos...but now he's gone."

"He'll be back."

She didn't answer.

"You're safe here." He sat back down, kitty-corner from her.

"Safe?" She looked at him sadly, shook her head.

"He came, Sara."

"You didn't give him a chance. I tried really hard, and you fucked it up for me." She stood. "Someone's going to die."

Abe was quiet, rubbing the groove on his desk with his index finger. He looked up at her. "All I know to do, Sara, is to try my best to understand what you're saying. I believe you mean what you say. But I don't always know what to do. And I have to rely on my own best judgment. Your arm was bleeding. I had to take care of that."

"You're a nice man." She looked at him, sadly. "But it's too late."

◆◆◆

Corey's office was in an older building overlooking Elliot Bay. The stone building had once been a hardware emporium. She turned to face the Sound. From her seventh floor window, she could see Blake Island, a deep green mound framed by dark gray seas and shifting, pale gray skies.

The buzzer was softer than it used to be; she'd made some minor office improvements. Corey went through her sparse reception area. The half-glass door said: Corey Logan, in big block letters. Framed in the window, she recognized Rosa, Snapper's mom. Rosa had come from Eastern Washington, near Yakima, where they raised horses. Corey had called her yesterday, and Rosa had insisted on catching the first bus this morning.

"You look tired," Corey said when they were comfortably seated in her office.

"It's nothing." Rosa was short, plainly dressed in a white blouse and a blue skirt, with every jet-black hair in place. She was well-groomed, almost formal—no, demure; that was the word. Corey knew otherwise. Her parents had come from Mexico to work illegally in the apple orchards. At sixteen, she'd married a rough-hewn horse breeder. Snapper was born a year later. From the get-go, there was tension between Snapper and his father, Rawley Parker. The friction turned violent over Snapper's sexual orientation. Snapper ran away when he was sixteen. Corey found him at seventeen, and hid him from his angry father. Rosa had stepped up for her boy, stood toe to toe with his dad, never wavering.

"Rosa, Snapper's—I'm sorry—Bud. I forget you call him Bud. He's back in Seattle. I'm trying to find him. I called you because I thought you might be able to help me. I know Bud keeps in touch with you. You didn't have to come all this way though."

"I did. I want to see him. I want to tell him he can come home. Thanks to God." Rosa crossed herself with three fingers. "His father is not so angry anymore. Rawley had his accident, with the horses, and he can't walk very well. It made him want his boy back. It was a miracle." She nodded, somber. "Also, I'm guessing that horse kicked him a good one—" Rosa made a fist. "—bam, right in the head." When Corey fought back a grin, Rosa's smile turned to a laugh. "Had to help."

Corey brightened, laughing too, then turned serious. "I'm sorry about Rawley's accident." Corey paused. "I know how happy Bud will be, though, about his dad's change of heart," she offered, meaning it.

"I hope so…" Rosa smiled, remembering something. "He sent me a postcard, from California. That was four weeks ago. It was the first time in almost a year." She showed Corey the postcard, smiling surfers riding the waves. On the back it said, "Dear mom, Good things breaking soon. As ever, your loving son, Bud."

Corey felt her mood shifting, something about the card.

"I don't know where to find him. Here, or in California. I don't even know the names of his friends," Rosa explained sadly. "But I will help you, even if it is only to run errands or drive you places."

Corey went around her desk. "Do you have a place to stay?"

"To me, this city could be New York or Paris. I don't know anything."

Corey wrote down the name of a motel. "This place is clean and safe. I'll call you later, say five, and we'll look for Bud together. By then, I should have some leads."

When Rosa left, Corey sat at her window, her boots up on the sill.

◆◆◆

Olympic had an open campus, and students were allowed to sign out. Amy lived nearby, and she'd invited Billy to help her with her architecture project during their midday lunch and free period.

Amy had an airy second floor bedroom. Billy and Amy were lying side-by-side on the blue and white quilt that covered her bed. Their clothes were strewn on the floor. "Show me what you like," Billy whispered. "I want to make you happy."

"I like you," she whispered back and put her tongue in his ear. Before he could think what to do she was kissing his neck, then his chest. He wasn't sure she understood what he meant. Maybe she had. But now he was so excited he worried he'd have an orgasm before they even started.

He almost came when she helped him put the condom on. She just knew how to do it, so it was really sexy. After, she slowed down, kissing his face and lips, while he played with her. She put his hands between her legs, helped him find the right spot. Pretty soon she was moaning, holding him really tight, and then she started shaking. Was she having an orgasm already? It could be one, but he wasn't sure. He worried then, that maybe it was over, and he was too late. But when she was finished, she just took his penis, spread some kind of slippery lubricant on the condom, then slowly slid it inside of her. As he entered her, she gasped. After that, it was everything he'd ever hoped for.

When it was over, he kissed her tenderly then watched her smile. He was wondering what to say now—if he should tell her it was perfect, thank her, or what. Did she know that he'd only done this with one other girl? And only a few times. It was with Morgan. And last time was maybe three months ago—no, it was three months he'd been telling himself it was three months ago. So maybe six months. Yeah, she had to know that he was like a total beginner, that he didn't really know how to do this.

Did she actually come? Wasn't that supposed to be harder? She was still underneath him. He couldn't even remember exactly how that happened. He rolled beside her. "Was that okay?" he finally asked, a little sheepish.

"Hmm," she settled in. "You like it?"

"Are you kidding?" He looked at her. "Could you tell it was, uh—you know—pretty quick."

Amy ran her tongue along his lower lip. "My first time, ever. I thought it would be, you know, harder. It hurt at first, but then it was really sweet."

"What?" Billy looked at her, eyes wide, confused. "Your first time?"

"Hmm-hmm. You're my first lover, ever."

"But you were so popular?"

"So? That doesn't mean I made love with any of those guys."

"Jeez. I had no idea. If I'd known—"

"If you'd known, you would have been way too careful. I know *you*, Billy Logan Stein. That's why I didn't tell you."

"Maybe, yeah, I guess you do." Billy smiled at her; she was so smart.

"Well I never would have guessed that. I thought you were so—I dunno—experienced."

"Well, you don't know everything then." She held him to her. "How about this? In a little while, we can do it again."

Billy gently stroked her hair, speechless.

When Sara left Abe's office, she didn't know where to go. All she knew was that she'd missed her chance and that bad things were going to happen. She'd called her dad, hoping he'd take her out for lunch. But he was at the hospital, doing something important. She took the bus to Broadway, then went north, down Tenth, until she saw her school, the Olympic Academy. She had to warn her friends.

The "campus" of the Olympic Academy covered over an acre, on Tenth. It was a landscaped cluster of structures, five in all, anchored in the middle by the Arts and Humanities building, a five story, 50,000 square foot affair. The "Ah Hoo building," as it was often called, was teal green, with huge windows that revealed classrooms, a dance studio, the wood shop, and a group of plexiglass teachers' offices. Inside, the supply lines were plexiglass. The design committee's notion was that the kids would see and understand the wiring, plumbing, heating, and so forth. The sewage lines, however, were painted sea blue.

Sara walked right to the fir-framed front door. Last summer, the corridors at Olympic had been vandalized. Since then, the smoky glass doors locked automatically. She'd given up her ID card when she was suspended, so she couldn't even open the automatic doors. Instead, she rang the buzzer. Sara knew the elderly receptionist with the frosty hair and tight smile would see her on the video monitor, and she tried to smile winningly at the camera. A few minutes later, Owen Sentor stepped outside.

"Sara, can I help you?"

"I need to see my friend, Randy."

"School's in session, and I'm sure he's in class."

Sara checked the time on her iPhone. "He's probably in art history. Could you get him for me please?"

"Is this an emergency, Sara?"

"Definitely. I reached Apollo. Someone's going to die. I need to talk with Randy, right away."

"Sara, we've been through this already. I can't interrupt class for these anxieties. I'll call Dr. Stein if you'd like."

"Can I come in? Please? Talk with him in the hall? It'll just take a minute."

"I'm sorry Sara. You can't take him out of class. But come in and wait while I call your doctor."

"You're not listening." Sara turned and left, muttering, "May Zeus, the lightning-bearer, strike you dumb as you are deaf."

At a bench on Tenth, she sat and called Abe. She wasn't sure why she was calling him, but she was really scared now and didn't know whom else to call. When she got his voice mail, she hung up.

Sara walked around the school. In the alley, behind the Olympic campus, she lit a fire in a trashcan. She began chanting, her own hastily, home brewed stew—fashioned from a beginner's knowledge of occult practices and her more elaborate understanding of Greek mythology. She asked for protection for her friends. From Evil. From the Beast. Nothing very specific. Just a prayer to ward off she-wasn't-sure-what.

◆◆◆

When the phone rang, Corey was still looking out the window, feeling wired and worried. The thing that was bothering her—that Billy wasn't "popular"—was odd, irrational. "Totally out there," as Billy would say. For christsake, he didn't seem to care. Still, something was wrong—broken— at Olympic. The phone kept ringing. She hoped it would be Abe—he knew to call on the second line—and she was surprised to hear the voice of her old friend, Lieutenant Lou Ballard.

"Hey, Lou. I forget you have this number. What's up?"

"I need you down here at Volunteer Park. Something you should see."

She knew she'd never get anything more from Lou on the phone. "On my way."

Ten minutes later she was driving her black pick-up off Prospect, past the water tower, around the reservoir. She parked in front of the Seattle Asian Art Museum, finding a space between two double-parked police cars. Police business was usually easy to find, and Corey followed its brazen signs, walking west toward Federal, coming down to the crime scene. The police had gathered around a clump of trees, easily accessed from the street below.

She saw her friend Lou coming up the hill to meet her. He'd recently made lieutenant and lost a little weight. Still, he was built like a pear, and his ever-present tie was almost always too thin. "This is lousy," were the first words out of his mouth.

"Okay," Corey said, bracing herself. "Why am I here, Lou? Topic sentence please."

Lou rubbed the bald spot on his head. "He had your phone number in his wallet."

Her pulse quickened and her stomach tensed up, taking orders from some part of her brain that she couldn't control.

"I want to see." She followed him down the hill.

Lou took her down the hill, to the body in the bushes. The man was lying on his back. His hands were beside his head, fingers spread, as if he'd been posing for a picture. The knuckles were swollen, battered and bruised. He had the battered, scarred face of an aging boxer after a recent fight. His nose had been broken, long ago. His ears were misshapen, his face was cut and bruised, and his eyelids and brow were layered with scars. The man had a thin black mustache, and a prominent scar that went from his cheek over a partially closed eye then rose onto his brow and forehead. He had black, curly hair. Corey leaned in closer, saw that his face had been very skillfully made-up, and the curly black hair was actually a top-of-the-line wig. This was a boy's face, artfully made to look like an older man. "How?" she asked.

"The makeup? Who knows. He used a fancy makeup appliance." Lou pointed out the edge of the foam latex appliance. It blended seamlessly with his skin at his brow. "I'd say he OD'd, though. Can't tell for sure. There's no sign of a struggle. Even the knuckles, that's makeup."

Corey kneeled beside the hand. It too, had been skillfully worked on. The bruises and twisted knuckles weren't real.

"Another weird thing." Lou wore latex gloves. He gently opened the man's mouth, lifted his tongue. There was an old silver coin under the dead man's tongue.

"Jesus," Corey whispered. "What's that about?"

"No idea. It must be part of some ritual." Lou shrugged. "Yeah, I'm betting he OD'd, that the coin and the makeup are part of some kind of screwy ceremony gone bad. We'll do an autopsy." He adjusted his thin tie. "The makeup's really expert...top drawer...figure that..." Lou cracked a knuckle. "You know him?"

She looked closer. It was hard to tell under the elaborate makeup. It began with the skillfully-crafted mask, then the makeup was layered on, every line, every feature its own project. It was, she realized, both gaudy and grotesque. She lifted a chain, hanging from the boy's neck. It carried a small silver stallion. Jesus. Oh shit. Her face went white. "Oh, no. Oh God." She felt Lou's arm around her, keeping her up.

"One of yours?" he asked, quiet.

"Uh-huh. Agh. His name's Snapper—No, no...it's Bud, Bud Parker." Corey stared at Snapper's once-handsome face, and she began to cry.

CHAPTER FIVE

"Motherfucker." Sara spit it out. "You stupid, time-wasting, useless, motherfucker."

Abe watched her pace furious circles in his office. She was crying and railing, going in and out of the present. He had no idea what she was so upset about. "What have I done?" he asked, again.

"I told you about the Horseman. Murdered on the Isthmus Road. I told you. You weren't listening. I told you. I told you!"

What had she told him, he wondered. "Please tell me again."

"Sciron hurled the Horseman from the great white rock into the sea. He made him wash his feet, then he threw him from the rock to the giant green turtle who was waiting to devour him. I told you this. Are you deaf? I told you!" And she started crying.

Abe hesitated. "Yes, you did tell me. But it's a myth that goes back thousands of years. I don't see why it's suddenly so upsetting." When she ignored him, he added, "I'm sorry. I don't understand."

"That's because you're not listening," she screamed. "Stupid, useless, time-waster. Why don't you pay attention? Why didn't you do something?" Sara slumped to the floor, head in her hands, sobbing now.

As Abe waited, she began chanting, calling on Theseus. Something about Medea and her poison. Then she was rambling about the Horseman—Theseus' charioteer—and the Isthmus road.

He had an idea. "Sara, I'm trying to listen. But I'm confused about something. Will you please tell me how the Horseman died."

"Will you just listen?"

"I will."

She took a beat, steadying herself. "Poison. Wolfsbane. Medea's poison," she whispered.

"Poisoned?"

"Wolfsbane. It started as the deadly foam scattered by the slavering mouths of Cerberus, the three-headed hellhound that guards the gates to Hades, when Hercules dragged him out of the Underworld. It lives on bare rocks. It's the deadliest of poisons."

"When?"

"Last night. The Beast has risen. He became Sciron to kill the Horseman, using Medea's poison."

She was taking fragments from different stories, combining them.

"He's on the move, ravaging, playing with me, unstoppable."

She was back to the present. Good. "Where did the Horseman die Sara?"

"The park."

"Where?"

"Volunteer Park."

What? Jesus. God. There it was. "Bud? Bud Parker?" he asked, incredulous.

She shook her head, no. "Don't you know anything?" she wailed, and Sara kept crying, refusing to look at him.

"Snapper?" he tried again.

She made a little noise. "The Horseman."

Abe put it together. "Snapper's the Horseman?"

Sara took the black damascene silver stallion from around her neck, raised it to show him. "The Horseman's dead. The Beast has risen. The Beast has killed my friend. I told you that."

Abe just stared at her. He remembered Corey telling him how Snapper was raised on a horse farm. How had she predicted this? How could he be so far behind her? "How do you know Snapper?" he eventually asked.

Sara just shook her head, side to side. "The Beast killed the Horseman. No one would listen." She said it over and over.

When she was quiet again, Abe said, "The police say Snapper—the Horseman—died of an overdose."

"Poisoned. Wolfsbane, Medea's poison." She shook her head, side to side. "Just listen, if you can."

"Wolfsbane?" he asked.

"The poison she used when she tried to kill Theseus, at a feast hosted by King Aegeus of Athens. Aegeus saved Theseus—at the very last moment—when he recognized his sword and realized he was his own son."

Abe had read the story, and in fact, the spot where the cup fell is still on display on the floor of the Dolphin Temple.

"When her plan to poison Theseus failed, Medea fled. She cast a magic cloud around herself. No one could see her. The Beast has dark powers, like Medea. He can take many forms. He can be Sciron or Cerberus the hellhound or even the Minotaur. And when he wants to disappear, the Beast can cast a magic cloud, too."

"Who's the Beast?" Abe tried.

"He's killing my friends. I need Theseus to help. Help me find Theseus. Listen to me and help me." She raised her eyes. "Please."

He went around his big desk, took her hand, then her elbow, leading her to the chair. When she was seated, Abe leaned against the front edge of his desk, facing her. "I will, Sara. I will listen to you. Very carefully. I promise." Abe nodded, still dumbstruck by her prescient knowledge of Snapper's death. She'd predicted it. And he hadn't actually believed her when she said someone was about to die—at least not literally, in the present. No, he hadn't really heard her; she was right about that. "How did you know Snapper?" he asked, leaning back against the edge of his desk.

"The Horseman was Theseus' friend. I'm sure he came back to help me. I got a postcard. On the front there was a beautiful wild stallion. On the back it just said, 'Coming soon. Our secret.' He didn't say when. I was going to warn him. Before I could find him, the Beast struck him down."

"How could you know he was in danger? I'm not doubting you, Sara, I simply don't understand."

"My time-waster shrink. I'll show you what I know. When they found the Horseman's body, did he have an old coin in his mouth?"

"Yes, under his tongue. How—"

"It's an obolus," she interrupted. "It's payment for Charon, the ferryman of Hades, who carries souls of the dead across the river Styx that divides the world of the living from the world of the dead."

"How—?"

"Please don't keep asking that."

"I'm sorry, but please bear with me. Can you tell me more?"

"Upon death, the soul leaves the corpse and takes the shape of the former person. Hermes leads the dead soul to the entrance of the underworld where Charon's boat is waiting. Only those who pay with the coin are ferried across. Those that can't pay the fee are trapped between two worlds, left wandering the shore. After the boat ride, souls enter through the gates. Cerberus, the ferocious hellhound, still guards the gates. Hercules returned the monster safely to Hades. Cerberus allows all souls to enter, but none to leave. The Beast left the coin to insure that the Horseman would be trapped forever in the Underworld."

Abe raised his hand, impressed. "I had no idea..."

"Here's a way for you to think about it. It's from a song my mother used to like. Do you remember 'Hotel California'? It's from your day..."

Abe frowned. "Eagles?"

"Right. Yeah... Here's how it ends...." Sara began singing, in a soft, sweet voice. "Last thing I remember, I was running for the door...I had to find the passage back to the place I was before... Relax, said the night man, we are programed to receive...you can check out anytime you like, but you can never leave..." She smiled, sadly. "That was for the Horseman."

Abe was moved by Sara's unexpected pairing of the Eagles and the Underworld, and by her lovely, haunting, singing voice. "Thank you for that, Sara, I didn't know you could sing so well."

"You're the first grown up ever heard me sing—except my mom and dad when I was little."

"I'm honored, you're quite a gifted young lady."

"Then why won't anyone listen to me?"

"I'm listening. Believe me...and I'm remembering some other lyrics from that same song. 'They gathered for the feast...they stab it with their steely knives... But they just can't kill the beast...'"

"Very good, doctor."

"Can I ask another question?"

She shrugged. "It's what you do."

"Fair enough...Snapper—the Horseman—was made up to look like a battered older man. An aging, scarred, boxer. Do you know why?"

"The makeup is likely a death mask. It could be a send off to the underworld. I'm guessing the Beast pictures Tartarus, the great abyss."

"Tartarus?"

"The worst place the judges at the gates can send a soul. Cyclopes and Sisyphus are imprisoned there. It's a prison of eternal torment and suffering." Sara made a sad face.

"Why?"

"I'm not sure about that. The Beast is growing stronger, working his dark magic—telling us something."

"What?"

"I don't know. He's some kind of freak—a freak who likes showing off. The boxer has some kind of meaning for him. But I'm guessing he simply doesn't care what we think. He's flaunting his power. Telling us that he's unstoppable."

"Unstoppable?"

"Imagine Phaea, the Crommyonian Sow, a monstrous wild pig that ravaged an entire region. Unstoppable until Theseus killed her. Or Cerberus, the three-headed Hellhound with a serpent's tail and a mane of snakes. It took Hercules to best him. Or the Minotaur, a child-eating monster. All unstoppable without a divine hero. Do you understand?"

"I'm starting to."

"Yes. That's why we need Theseus...the Horseman is dead because I couldn't find him."

"Did the Horseman know the Beast?"

She ignored him, fingering a spike on her collar. She was off somewhere, crying again.

"Sara, this is important. I understand that we need to find a modern-day Theseus to slay the Beast. But to do that we also need to know the Beast."

Sara turned her head away from him.

"Can you describe the Beast?" he tried again.

"No," she whispered. "No."

"Sara, do you have any ideas? Possibilities?"

"No. No. No," she screamed, flailing her arms. "You're not helping. You're hurting."

Abe watched her as she started to cry again, aware that she was right.

◆◆◆

"How could she possibly know that?" Corey asked Abe after he'd explained that Sara had predicted Snapper's death.

They were at the Queen City Grill, one of the most beautiful rooms in the city. Something about the dark woods, the splendid mullioned windows, the handsome bar, the muted colors and the organization of the space and light gave the busy restaurant an aura all its own, a warm, welcoming glow.

It was 6:30 and Corey and Abe were having a drink at a black-painted wood booth in the back. Abe sipped a single malt scotch. Corey had a Bombay Blue Sapphire Gin Martini.

"She knew he was in danger before he died. She warned me. And now, she insists he was poisoned. At this point I'm inclined to believe her."

"I'm still not understanding."

"In Sara's mythological universe, Snapper was the Horseman, Theseus' charioteer. She kept telling me that the Horseman was in danger, that she had to find Theseus to save him. I didn't understand what she meant. She kept saying I wasn't listening. And to the extent that she meant that I wasn't hearing her, she was right. She told me, and I simply didn't get it. Babe, you understand confidentiality, so you know I can't tell you any of the specifics, but Sara knew. She predicted it. And I let her down." Abe raised a big palm, nodding sadly. He nursed his Glenmorangie.

Corey was frowning, rubbing the bridge of her nose with thumb and forefinger. Abe sat back, watching her. She looked at him. "Could this be some sort of weird coincidence? Or could she have overheard something? I mean how could she predict something like this?"

"She knew about the coin in his mouth. She even explained what it meant."

"What does it mean?"

"You know I can't talk about that."

"Okay…okay, I get that…so just break it down for me, however you can…"

"I'll try…" Abe leaned in. "I think there are two distinct pieces to this. One is keeping anyone else—including Sara—from getting hurt. The second is helping Sara get well. And of course, they're entangled in an impossibly intricate knot, as hard for me to untangle as—I dunno—the Gordian knot."

"You're making me feel uneducated."

"Sorry. It was a knot tied by Gordius, king of Phrygia, so intricate that it was said that it could only be untied by the future ruler of Asia. Alexander ended up cutting the rope with his sword."

"And that awful phrase, 'thinking outside the box' was born."

"Smart, sassy and literate—quite perfectly literate, in everything I've ever felt was important." Abe looked at her, in that loving way that only he could do it.

She took his hand, plainly enjoying his gaze, then she shifted gears. "Please tell Lou whatever you can that's relevant to the case."

Abe nodded. "Of course, I will."

"And if you agree, let's you and I start with the second piece—helping Sara get well. It's what you know."

"Yes…and the starting point has to be that I'm worried about her, really worried. She has some kind of toxic knowledge. And at least one of her friends has died. I know that she's suffering, blaming herself, but I don't have any idea how to even access this poison. Put simply, the therapy isn't working. I don't know what to do."

"So how can I help?"

"I'd like your help to figure out how I can reach Sara. You know more about kids than anyone I know."

"Tell me what you can."

"I can't bring her into the present. She tells me stories from Greek mythology that are invested with present day meaning, but I can't get her to connect them to the present. She's terrified, haunted by something, and it's tormenting her—and she doesn't even know what she knows. Though she's courageously fighting it in the past, it's more than she can bear. I worry that if I can't reach her, she'll lose whatever fragile connection to reality that she has. She's smart and brave, but Sara's hanging on by her fingernails."

"Then follow her into the past...any way that you can...in my experience, to reach a young person, you have to go where they live. Even if it's hard and illogical. *Where they live.* There's no other way."

"Well Sara lives in ancient Greece, and truthfully, I don't know how to get there."

"Let her take you there. She knows the way. And then, when she trusts you, even a little, you can gently take her hand and lead her back. You're very good at that."

Abe squeezed her hand. "I'll try, babe. I'm just not sure how."

"When I found Jolene, after Teaser whipped her with a red-hot coat hanger, *she still wanted him back.* She said her time with him, when she was eleven, was her best time. I wouldn't go there. I wouldn't let her have that. I was just too angry. And I lost her forever."

Abe took her hand across the table, nodded. He remembered how when Jolene took her own life, she had Corey's business card in her pocket.

"I should have accepted her reality. No questions, no hesitation. Just gone with it. I'll regret that I didn't for the rest of my life."

"Point taken." He found her eyes. "I'm lucky to have you. Sara's lucky I have you. I'll do what I can."

"I know you, babe. *What you can* will be enough."

◆◆◆

When she looked up the hill from Federal Avenue, Sara could see the crime scene. She'd walked north from her house, carrying what she needed in her shoulder bag. And there it was, right where it was supposed to be. She'd half hoped that they'd cleaned it up. That she could do her work wherever she wanted. But no, the leftover yellow tape was in plain view, marking just where the body was found. Sara knew what she had to do. Just being here made her want to cry though. And she did, as she made her way up the hill from the street. She climbed through the bushes, pushing aside the wide yellow tape. The bushes hid a little clearing. In the protected area, she could picture what the Beast had done. Carried the body down from his car. Laid it out proudly, so his work would be admired. The makeup was bothering her. What was that about? Perhaps it was just a whim, something to divert attention from his real purpose. More likely, it was a death mask, a special send off to the underworld that had a special meaning for him, for him alone. What she wondered, was that?

Sara forced herself to the task at hand. She was here to say goodbye to her friend. First, she set the ritual fire. Then she began laying out what she'd brought. There was a book, a post card, an old T-shirt. Her bag was full of things that reminded her of the Horseman. As she set out a picture of him teaching her to ride, she was interrupted by a gruff voice.

"What the hell?" the policeman asked. He wore a yellow raincoat and had a potbelly.

Sara realized it was drizzling. "The person they found here was my friend. I've come to say good bye."

"Look. You don't belong here. You can't make fires here. And you sure as hell can't do any kind of voodoo shit here."

Sara began gathering her things. There was no point trying to explain herself. It occurred to her that she was going to jail. "Call Dr. Abe Stein," she said. "He'll explain."

"At the station, you can call whoever you want."

◆◆◆

"Eenee, meenee, minee, mo, catch the sweetie by the toe..." Minos was saying in a soft, singsong voice as he checked out Alex's room. On the walls there were pictures of redheaded Randy, Lucky Red, everywhere. The game wasn't really fun, today. Un-unh. The getting in part was okay. It made his heart pump pretty fast. And the little house in Ravenna was kind of fun to check out. Sweet on the inside. He liked how Lucky Red's lover boy had two moms. And how they had these pictures of themselves all over the place. He didn't like the naked ones in the bedroom, though.

"He has two mommies, go boy go. Einee meenee minee mo." Minos laughed at his little rhyme. The fun had stopped when he got to Alex's room. Yeah. He couldn't find anything, anywhere. Even worse, he wasn't sure what to look for. Something Snapper had given to Randy. A book. Something inside the book? Something he said?

Minos checked himself out in the mirror. Under his black leather greatcoat, he was dressed entirely in black. He checked his hair, his scar, his birthmark. Perfect. The Master would appreciate that. He touched the purple stain on his left cheek, worried, now, that the Master would be angry if he didn't find Snapper's gift to Randy. The Master didn't like loose ends and this was a big one. "Einee meenee minee mo, Master's angry... No, no, no!" he whispered. But how could he find it if he didn't even know what he was looking for? Snapper said he had some kind of proof, he knew that much...

Minos faced the mirror, poised, working hard to put the Master out of his mind. He framed his face with both thumbs and forefingers. When he felt steady, and silky on the inside, he began his slow, silent dance. He curled his fingers into fists, slow-motion shadowboxing, finding his marks in the air, then he swayed his body, graceful and deliberate, as he uncurled his fingers until the extended forefinger of each hand settled just above his temples, curling forward, the Cretan Bull.

It was said that the Athenian king, Aegeus, sent Minos' son, Androgeus, to fight the same white bull that sired the Minotaur, and Androgeus was killed. Outraged, Minos waged war on the Athenians. When the war dragged on, Minos prayed to his father, Zeus, to avenge Androgeus' death. Zeus punished the Athenians with earthquakes and famine. When the distraught Athenians consulted the Delphic Oracle, they were told to give Minos whatever he wanted. He demanded tribute of seven Athenian youths and seven virgin maidens every lunar year to be fed to the Minotaur.

The Cretan Bull could be as fierce, as ferocious, as merciless, as the Minotaur.

Minos danced out from under the black cloud of the Master's anger.

◆◆◆

Billy and Amy were sitting around the kitchen table talking with Amy's mom, Connie Henderson. Connie was hoping to start an Olympic parent pledge for their house and others to be drug and alcohol free. This is not the first time they'd talked about it. Amy, who hated this idea, had asked Billy to be part of the conversation.

"It's a way for parents to know where it's safe for our children," Connie explained. She'd just come in from the garden, and she wore jeans and a sweatshirt. Connie was an older version of Amy, with long black hair, and plainly the source of Amy's gamine-like beauty. Connie was divorced from Amy's father, a prominent lawyer, and she and Amy shared this big Federal Avenue home together.

"No, it isn't," Amy said. "You can't legislate abstinence. If kids want to drink or take drugs, they'll just do it in their cars. Besides, we're like totally unpopular already. This is nothing but trouble for us." Angry now, Amy's cheeks flushed a little bit red. Billy thought it made her look even more intense, and—what was that *Cat-on-A-Hot-Tin-Roof* word? Sultry, yeah. Sultry.

"Popular or not was your choice." Connie shot her daughter a look; this was plainly a sore subject. "Either way, we can set standards," Connie pointed out.

"Are you doing this for me or for you?" Amy asked.

"For both of us, all of us," Connie said. "It's a way for our community to come together around keeping our children safe."

"Community. What community?" Amy asked, redder still.

"You don't have to like everyone in it to be part of a community."

Billy leaned in, pensive. "I think what Amy means is that in a community that works, people communicate with each other. Accept differences. Look out for one another. Work things out. That's not Olympic."

Amy put a hand on his forearm, nodding. "Right. At Olympic, they tell you how to be, but no one does anything when someone is bullied or when someone is regularly excluded. At Olympic, most of the kids are scrambling for any kind of attention, a hand out, from a small group of popular kids. What kind of a community is that?"

"And parents, however well meaning, hoping to create a drug and alcohol free community for their children at Olympic have no chance of succeeding." Billy raised a palm. "None. It's only going to make everyone angry."

"Billy and I don't use hard drugs. We drink some wine and occasionally smoke pot. But we do it responsibly. Why can't you leave well enough alone?"

"You know I don't approve of any drug use or of underage drinking."

"One day it won't be your decision—"

Billy took Amy's hand, interrupting. "Mrs. Henderson—"

"Connie, please—"

"Connie, aren't you glad that you have a daughter who tells you what she does? Most of the kids at Olympic don't ever talk to their parents."

"Yes, I do like that. I still worry though." And after a beat, "Do you talk about these things with your parents?"

"Yes, absolutely."

"What do they say?"

"We talk a lot about good judgment. About when it's okay to drink or smoke dope. When it's safe. We talk about when it's important to say what you really feel and when you should hide it. We even talk about when it's okay to lie. What my mom and dad want is for me to exercise good judgment, reliably, and to talk with them when I don't know what to do. In the end, though, they leave it up to me."

"And that works?"

"We're getting there."

"*Reliably*? That's setting the bar pretty high."

Amy nodded. "Wouldn't you like me to try for that, even if it's hard? Billy and I talk about stuff, especially if one of us has a problem, and I would like to talk more with you, if you'd just be more respectful of my point of view. But whether we agree or not, at the end of the day, isn't the point for me to learn to make good decisions on my own?"

"I'll take that…" Connie touched her daughter's hand. "I'm sorry you feel that Olympic isn't working."

Amy took her mother's hand. "It can be a mean-spirited place. Why don't you talk with parents about fixing that? I think you'll find that they don't have a clue about what their children are thinking or doing or how they're treating each other."

Connie sat back. "OK. Point taken." And looking them over. "You two are good together."

◆◆◆

"And what am I supposed to do about Billy, anyway?" Sara was pacing in front of Abe's desk. "It freaks me out that you're his dad."

"I have to talk with you about that. Owen Sentor told another mom, who told Billy's mom, who said something to Billy last night."

"Shit. This sucks. I thought this was between us. Period."

"What goes on here is between us and stays between us unless you say otherwise. I can't control what people like Owen do, though he made a mistake, and I'll talk with him about it."

Sara was quiet, looking down.

"You could talk with Billy."

"Are you crazy? That would just freak *him* out."

"I doubt that, but it's up to you."

Sara sat back into the big leather chair. She crossed her legs underneath her, covered her face with both hands.

"Is talking about Billy upsetting you?" Abe gently asked.

Sara shook her head, no, and crying softly now, she whispered, "The Horseman is dead."

"Snapper?"

"The Horseman," she insisted. "Poisoned...my fault." She wiped her tears from her face, frustrated now, shaking her head back and forth. "And there's more danger every minute. The Beast is rising, getting stronger."

He believed her. "Would you like to talk with the police? I know a very able and trustworthy lieutenant."

"No. No. No! I tried that. I went to the station. They wouldn't listen. They wanted to take me to the hospital. They can't find the Beast. They can't even see the Beast."

"Can I help?"

"How can you help? You sap my strength."

"I'd like to help you feel safe—at least here in my office."

"I'd like to be safe."

"Would you like to make a safe place, right here?"

"Are you tricking me?"

"Try me."

Sara stood, and taking a magic marker from her bag, she drew a large black circle—almost seven feet in diameter—on Abe's beige carpet. She eyed Abe, waiting for him to protest. When he didn't, Sara drew a five-pointed star in the circle. At each point she set a candle. She began chanting, setting her candles around the circle, then lighting them.

Abe watched her.

When she was satisfied with her circle, Sara reached into the bag for her dagger. She raised her Athame high. "I am the priestess, secret sister of Theseus, I pray to Apollo. I call on blue-haired Poseidon, master of ships and stallions, you who sired him, lead me to Theseus. The Beast is rising. I need him now." Sara sat in her circle, set her Athame on the floor in front of her. She reached into her bag and took a vial of her homemade wine ambrosia, drank it down, then she raised both hands high and closed her eyes.

Abe waited until she was settled in—taking long, slow breaths—then he stepped in to her magic circle and sat beside her. After a moment he turned to her. "Let's go back together. Please tell me about Theseus again," he asked. "Anything you think is important…"

"Theseus, the son of Poseidon, the earth shaker…and son of Aegeus the king…Aethra, his mother lay with both the man and the god on the same night." She paused. "Poseidon conceded paternity to Aegeus, but I believe Poseidon was also Theseus' father. Can you imagine? Fathered by a man and a god?" The corners of her mouth turned up, almost a smile." Theseus ran away when he was eighteen. He had special gifts—he was not only fearless and strong, he was wise and compassionate. He crossed the Isthmus to Athens. Theseus killed all of the thieves on the

Isthmus, making it safe for travelers. 'Serving them as they served others.' He threw Sciron from the great white rock into the sea."

Abe watched her, eyes shut, lost in her story. "Sciron killed the Horseman, didn't he?" he asked her.

"Sciron killed Theseus' charioteer, his childhood friend, Dexios, on the Isthmus, yes." She hung her head. "Dexios was his companion on his land route to Athens. Avenging him was the first of his great feats."

"Please go on."

"Theseus had many great triumphs." As she numbered them, she tapped her dagger on the carpet. "He killed the ferocious Minotaur in Daedalus' great labyrinth. At Crommyon, he hunted and killed the fierce and monstrous wild sow. He was the founder king of Athens, where he abolished the monarchy and declared Athens a democracy. He unified the scattered villages and gave aid to the weak and helpless. He sailed on the Argo to find the Golden Fleece. He befriended Peirithous, the reckless one, who foolishly stole his cattle. He saves his impetuous friend's life… time and again. If I can't find Theseus, who will save him now?"

She's confusing the chronology, Abe realized, and weaving bits and pieces from the present into these myths. "So Peirithous could be in danger now?"

"There is danger from the Beast if I don't find Theseus."

"Can we find Peirithous? Can we protect him?"

"I've told you how the Beast can become many, many terrifying monsters. Only Theseus can kill the beast. Only Theseus can protect his honorary twin, Peirithous."

She was giving the beast godlike powers, dark magic, shape-shifting—like Zeus, he could be a serpent, an eagle, a ferocious monster, even a white bull. "Sara, I'd like to see you every day for two hours. Until we find Theseus."

"The Gods aren't helping, they're not even listening. The Beast is making it impossible for me to reach the Oracle. I need strength. I need Apollo, I need Zeus, I need Poseidon. I don't need an absentminded, strength-sapping shrink. You're a nice man, and I think you're well-meaning, but you're not helping. Not at all. You don't even know how to help."

Sara shook her head, no, off somewhere, chanting again. "I am the priestess, secret sister of Theseus. I need him now." And louder still, "I need him now!" She put her hands on her face, crying again.

Abe spoke softly. "I'll help you find Theseus," he gently promised. "Let's try again tomorrow."

◆◆◆

Minos wore his long, black greatcoat. Over his left shoulder, he carried a black shoulder bag. The stain, the purple bloom covering his scar, spread across his cheek. He stood across the street from the Logan-Stein's house, watching. He looked down, studying a picture of Billy and Amy, the same picture he'd taken from Lucky Red's room.

Minos shuffled across the street, eyes down. When he passed the house he turned into an alley and doubled back. At the Logan Stein's back door, Minos rang the back door bell, twice, then he backed into the alley and hid behind a garage. After a few minutes, he went back to the door and used a tool to pick the lock. Minos checked out the kitchen then turned up the back stairs. He was thinking the game was getting better. He liked Billy's room, liked the soccer photos, the pictures of the tall, pretty girl. He went through the books on his desk. Nothing. Minos checked the bookshelf, carefully opening each book. Zero. Carefully, he went through Billy's closet, searching for he wasn't sure what. Nothing. He clenched his fists, shaking them in the air, then Minos touched the purple bloom on his cheek. Knowing that he must be punished for his failure, Minos pinched his scar, pressing down hard, until a tear flowed down his cheek.

He took a knife with a curved blade out from an inside pocket of his leather greatcoat. Next, he took a little box from the shoulder bag he carried. In the box there was a snake, a serpent. With one hand he held the serpent, writhing in front of him. With his knife, Minos cut the snake's head off. He set the head on the floor, in a pool of snake blood. He took a thin paintbrush from his shoulder bag. With the brush he drew the horns of the Cretan Bull in blood around the head of the snake. In the oak floor, Zeus's wood, he used his knife to carve Zeus's symbol, the thunderbolt, then he squeezed the headless snake, spreading blood in a dark-red circle around his sacrifice. As he drew his blood circle, Minos said a prayer, asking for help from the most powerful of all of the gods. When he was satisfied with his sacrifice, Minos turned, stared at his face in the mirror. He shook his fists in the air, wildly, hoping against hope that Zeus would answer his prayer.

CHAPTER SIX

"Gross," Billy muttered. "Really disgusting." He was sitting on his bed, looking down at the snake's head, set in the pool of blood on the floor. Abe and Corey were standing there staring at the grotesque who-could-say-what message left puddling on Billy's floor. Lou Ballard sat in the desk chair, shaking his head.

"Any idea what this is?" Lou asked Billy.

"No. None. Really gross," he repeated. "And whoever did this moved my stuff around." Billy pointed at the books on his desk.

"Yeah, they were looking for something. I'm guessing they left this when they couldn't find it," Lou explained.

"Those look like horns." Abe pointed at the lines painted in snake blood, then the crude sideways Z carved in the floor. "Is this some kind of symbol?"

"A gang deal?" Corey asked.

"If it is, I never saw anything like it," Lou replied.

"I have no reason to put these things together, but my gut tells me this is somehow connected to Snapper…it's got that same creepy weirdness." Corey nodded; she knew what she knew.

"The dead kid with the makeup?" Lou asked, confused.

"Yeah, Snapper…the Horseman…" Abe added.

"Horseman?" Lou scowled.

Abe didn't respond. He was studying the snakehead, the blood, the drawn horns, the crude sideways Z carved in the floor, and the larger blood circle that framed this grotesque display. Abe thought of Sara. "I have an idea," he offered. "I've been reading Greek mythology." Abe touched the carving in the floor. "The bull is an important symbol. And suppose this is a lightning bolt. What if this is some kind of sacrifice?"

"Maybe a cult?" Lou mused.

"Shit," Billy summed it up. He turned to his dad. "Sara might know what this is. It's the kind of thing she talks about."

"Who's Sara?" Lou wanted to know.

"Abe can't answer that," Corey explained. "But she's his patient."

"Shit is right," Lou said. "I'll talk with her."

"No you won't," Abe insisted; he had a tone. "I'll talk with Sara about it," he eventually offered. "After, I'll fill you in on anything that's relevant to the case." He frowned. "Lou, could you find out if Snapper was poisoned?" he asked, changing the subject.

"You already asked me to do that, twice. We didn't find anything. Is this patient of yours filling your head with all of these ideas about murder?"

"She believes he was poisoned with an ancient poison, wolfsbane. I think she's right...please ask your ME about that."

"Wolfsbane?" Lou shrugged. "Isn't that a band?"

Abe ignored him. "Did you find any drugs in his system?"

"No. The medical examiner is thinking some kind of freak accident—maybe he had a seizure, suffocated. I'd guess it was during some kind of weird ritual."

"So you don't know how or why he died?"

"We can always run some more tests."

"Thank you."

"I don't think this joker's coming back, but we'll leave a squad car here. Billy, stay home tonight. I'll put a man on you for the next twenty-four hours."

Billy made a face. "Can Amy come over?"

Corey nodded.

Billy pulled out his phone. Abe raised a palm. "How did Sara know Snapper?" Abe asked, working on something.

"Sara's brother, Peter, was a friend of his. They hung out with Randy and Alex some."

"Lou, do you have anything on Sara's brother, Peter Peterson?"

"I'll check, but I'm outta here. Every time I get around the Logan-Steins, you start telling me what I can and can't do, then, even more irritating, you start connecting things in ways that make no sense—"

"Lou, Snapper didn't kill himself, he wasn't in any ritual, weird or otherwise, and he sure as hell didn't make himself up to look like a badly-scarred, broken-down old boxer. And Abe can't tell you this but Sara, his patient, predicted Snapper's death. And she says he was poisoned. *This is all connected.*"

"Yes," Abe turned to Lou, who was already at the door, cracking his knuckles.

Lou turned back. "Lucky for you," he quipped. "I'm used to your *psycho-bullshit.*" He smiled meanly then let himself out.

◆◆◆

Sara was at Edge of the Circle Books, an occult bookstore on Pike at Boyleston. It described itself as "Seattle's resource for Paganism and the Occult." Sara had bought her Athame at this store, found helpful books on ceremonial magic, and she went often, especially when she was confused, as she was now.

She believed that the Beast had cast a spell, dark magic that was keeping her from reaching Apollo or Poseidon, not to mention Zeus. And without their help, she'd never find Theseus.

The gods were tricky, even touchy, she knew that much. Maybe she needed to make a sacrifice to Apollo? Hmm…that could be good.

Still something else was going on. It occurred to her that the Beast was using dark magic to hide Theseus—deflecting or redirecting her efforts in some weird way. So she was looking for books on psychic defense, self-protection, and dark magic. Yes, she needed to strengthen her defenses—fortify her magic circle—she was thinking, when she saw her father across the street waiting at a coffee shop.

Sara checked her watch. *Oh my god, I'm already fifteen minutes late.* She took a slow, calming breath, reminding herself that she wanted to do a good job with her dad. So why did she forget the time? Dark magic, slowing her down, fucking her up. She took another breath and hurried out of the store and crossed the street to meet her dad.

◆◆◆

Sara liked her dad's warm, bright smile when he stood up after he saw her coming in the café. She'd taken off her spiked collar, stowed it away in her shoulder bag, because she knew it bothered him. "Hey, Dad." Sara gave him a hug, then sat down beside him. She smiled, trying to make a good connection. "You wanted to see me?"

"Yes, I was hoping that if we met during the day, away from the house, maybe we could have a different kind of conversation."

"Different? How so?"

"I know you've been upset, and I know how you turn to your Greek myths and your magic at those times. But maybe today we could try less Greek mythology, less hocus pocus—no offense—try to be more scientific, more practical."

"I thought you loved Greek mythology. What about Hippocrates?"

"As you know, he's my idol. But that's because he was the first doctor to believe that diseases were caused naturally not because of superstition or punishment by the gods. And he's a real person, not a mythological figure. He focused on what was real. It's the opposite of what you're doing—weaving anxieties, fantasies and myths into some kind of classical Greek tragedy."

"That's like so totally unfair." Sara took a calming breath. This was already too hard. "People are dying. That's not anxiety, that's as real as it gets. And this conversation..." She raised her palms, lowered her head. "Is making things harder."

"OK." Jim took out his inhaler. Took a puff. "OK. Sorry. Let's start again... I love you, you know that...and I'd like to make things better. I'd like to help you get back on track. I'd like to see you feeling better, back in school."

"Me too...but I'm just so scared."

"Is Dr. Stein helping with that?"

"No. Not really. I don't think he can."

"Would you like the three of us to meet together?"

"No, no, I don't think that would work."

"Do you know just what it is that's scaring you?"

"You know. You know! The Beast is rising, he'll kill again, and I can't find Theseus."

"Is the Beast a person?"

"The Beast is a monster with powerful magic who can take so many forms. Sometimes the Beast is invisible."

"Sara, we talk about this all the time." Another puff. "I'm not sure how to help with this."

She took a moment, not wanting to screw it up again with her dad. He was one of the last people who cared about her. "There is something you could help with."

"Please. How can I help?"

"I'd like to talk with Peter..." She was sweating now, fidgeting.

"I think he could help. Can you reach him?"

"He's calling from the Greek Islands this week. When he does, I'll set up a call for you the next day." He nodded, pleased. "Yes, absolutely, let's do that."

"Yeah. Great. Really great. Thanks." Sara felt hot and her stomach was cramping.

"Are you alright?"

"No. I'm feeling dark magic. The Beast is using his dark magic on me."

"Sara, I'm worried about you. Do you want medication?"

She clenched her fists. "No... No... I want Theseus..."

"Theseus died thousands of years ago. You know that. I'm going to call Dr. Stein, and I'm going to recommend medicating you. This is worrying me. You're not alright."

She wiped her forehead with a napkin. "No, I'm not alright, Dad. I've been kicked out of school. The Beast is killing my friends. I have to stop him, except he's slowing me down at every turn. And no one is listening, *not even you...*"

"Sara, please..." Jim stood.

She walked past him, out of the café, a single tear flowing down her cheek, aware that the Beast's dark magic had really messed things up with her dad.

◆◆◆

"A snake's head in a pool of blood on your bedroom floor?" Amy's face was flushed. She held Billy's hand tightly. They were seated with Randy and Alex at the back of the Blue City Café. A policeman stood by the door.

"Yeah. Really crazy." Billy nodded, grimacing. "And it had these bull horns painted in snake blood and some kind of sideways Z carved underneath. And then there was a circle of blood all around it."

"I'm freaking out," Amy whispered in his ear. Then to the others, "Did you get hold of Sara?"

"She's on her way," Randy replied.

"It was so gross," Billy reiterated.

Randy and Alex listened attentively. Everyone was anxious, even Randy. Billy could tell.

Randy ran his hand through his wild red hair. "First the Snapper is somehow murdered—no way he'd kill himself and he's no druggie—then he's made up to look like a beat-up old boxer. Jesus, that is so freaky. Now this new weirdness."

"You're right about Snapper. He didn't OD," Billy added. "They didn't find any drugs in his system at the autopsy."

"I didn't say anything before, but I think someone went through all of the books in my room," Alex offered, serious. "Nothing I could prove but little things were moved. I pay attention to stuff like that."

"Shit, some creep is stalking us," Randy exclaimed.

"Why?" Amy wanted to know.

"I don't know. Snapper gave me a book to give to Sara if anything happened to him—and now it's gone. Missing."

"Does Sara know?"

"No. He made me promise not to tell anyone unless something happened to him. If I tell her now, and I don't have it, it will upset her even more. I thought I'd go through all of my things tonight—everything—and see if I can find it."

Randy saw Sara come through the door. "Hey Sara, over here." He waved her over.

Sara made her way to their table. She looked bad—disheveled, upset. It got worse when she saw Billy.

Billy stood, took her aside before she could sit down or turn away. "Look, I know you're seeing my dad. And this probably isn't the time to talk about it, but we have no choice."

"Why?"

"We need your help. We want to talk with you about something weird that just happened at my house. I think you may know what it means."

"What about your dad? Are you going to talk with him about me?"

"Only if you agree. Sara, we can manage this. I've been through it with my friend, Maisie."

"I've met her," Sara nodded. "She knows my brother. Your dad helped her, didn't he?"

"Yes, yes he did. Look my dad never says a word. And he's the best when there's danger."

Sara turned away. "Not so far," she muttered.

"Let's agree not to talk about him then. Okay?"

"Yeah, sure."

"Sara, it's easier than you imagine." Billy raised a palm. "Really. It's not a big deal. We'll talk more about it later. But right now we need your help. We think you're on to something. We think you're right—there *is* danger. Let me tell you why."

Sara nodded, visibly relieved. Billy pulled out a chair for her. "I'll help if I can," Sara volunteered.

Billy told her that someone had been breaking into their houses, going through their things, then he told her what he'd found in his room.

"Could you draw me a picture?"

Billy sketched a rough facsimile on a napkin.

"The Beast was in your room."

"Why do you think that?"

"Is your floor oak?"

"Yes, I think it is."

Sara began to sweat. "It isn't safe here. I need to make my circle. If you want my help, we'll have to go outside."

"Why?" Randy asked. But Sara was up and out the back door. The policeman was at the counter, buying a jelly doughnut. He had his back to them, and they left the café unnoticed.

They followed her to the alley behind the Blue City Café. Billy knew the spot. It was the same place where his mother had killed a man who was trying to kidnap him. After she shot him in the back of the head, they ran away, up the Inside Passage.

Sara set down her bag. She took out a piece of white chalk and drew a large circle in the alley, then with a piece of orange chalk, she drew a star inside her circle. The way she did it so quickly, Billy could tell she'd done this many times. They watched as she lit candles, performed her protective magic, and cast a spell to keep them safe. "We don't have much time," she said, worried. "The Beast is getting stronger."

"What does this have to do with the snake's head in Billy's room?" Randy wanted to know.

Sara looked down the alley, furtive. She still held Billy's makeshift drawing. "The snake's head was a sacrifice to Zeus. Oak is his wood. Zeus is known as the serpent god, often presenting himself as a serpent." She pointed to the sideways Z. "This is his thunderbolt. These look like the horns of a bull. Likely the Cretan Bull."

"Cretan Bull?"

Sara took a calming breath, checked out the alley. "Zeus became a snow white Bull to abduct Europa, the beautiful Phoenician princess, to Crete. Minos was their child. Years later, Minos called on Poseidon, who sent that same snow white bull from the sea. I believe that Zeus's white bull is the same bull as the Cretan beast that fathered the Minotaur..." Sara let this drift off, losing her focus.

"You really know this stuff. I had no idea," Billy said, encouraging her.

"Yes, I do," she confirmed, matter of fact. "Thank you for listening."

"I'm just not getting what it has to do with me. Please go on."

"Zeus later recreated the shape of the white bull in the stars, the constellation Taurus. The sacrifice in your room uses the Cretan Bull to appeal to Zeus." Sara took out her Athame, started chanting.

"Why would the Beast make a sacrifice?"

She took a breath. "He's angry about something, and he wants more power. He's looking for something. That's why he's going through your stuff. He hasn't found it and that's making him angry. I know he's using his dark magic to keep me from finding Theseus. Zeus is the most powerful of all the gods. The Beast will use whatever power Zeus grants him to keep us from reaching Apollo, from finding Theseus. He will stop at nothing."

"This is scaring me," Amy said.

"That's good. You have reason to be afraid," Sara said. "The Beast is going to kill again." Sara started chanting again, something about the Oracle and Theseus.

"You and your understanding of the Greek myths are very cool," Randy chimed in. "Still, I'm not convinced, all of this stuff is mythology. If it happened at all, it happened thousands of years ago. What does it have to do with us?"

Sara faced him. "You're careless and foolish, you need Theseus most of all."

"What?" Randy made a face. "Lighten up."

The policeman came out of the back door. He looked at Sara in her circle, her Athame raised high. "What the hell?" he yelled.

Sara hurriedly gathered her things and ran off, down the alley.

◆◆◆

Minos was in his lab, at his worktable. In the mirror he checked out his own makeup. It was more complex, and he was looking a little bit older. He wondered what that was about—something about his sacrifice to Zeus, he knew that much—though he didn't bother to figure it all out because he was feeling so good since the sacrifice. Yes, older on the outside and younger on the inside—at the same time—which was perfect. Minos was evolving, and he liked it. He'd actually asked for help with the snake's head, the blood, the Cretan Bull, and the thunderbolt. And Zeus, the sky god, had heard him. He knew that, too. He could feel Zeus's strength coursing through his veins, readying him to better serve the Master. The game had changed, though—because he'd left the sacrifice, they would know he'd been there. But that made him feel good too. So good that he sang a children's song. His game was getting more elaborate and he was happy he'd be playing again soon. The Master would feel better when he took Lucky Red. He sang, "Over the River and through the Woods to grandmother's house we go…" as he worked out his plan.

A picture of Randy was on a stand to his right. On his left side he'd set a scrapbook with pictures of the Cretan Bull. Minos had found, then organized, these photos when his father died. This scrapbook was chronological, and as Minos leafed through it, he frowned and stopped singing. The Cretan Bull grew older, and his face ever more battered, in each successive picture. He flipped back to an early picture of the Cretan Bull with his beautiful daughter Ariadne. She was four and her father held her hand. Their father was twenty-one and rakishly handsome then. He was a young boxer, his face still unscarred. Minos continued on, watching the Cretan Bull's face change as he continued fighting for the next sixteen years, more than fifty punishing fights. He paused at a picture of his "babaka" before his last big fight. The cuts and bruises were even worse than on Snapper's mask. He went on to a photo of the Cretan Bull's battered, bloodied face as he lay on his back on the canvas after his last fight, the fight that killed him. Minos resumed his song, "The horse knows the way to carry the sleigh through bright and drifty snow…" as he reached for the foam latex appliance he'd been working on for Lucky Red.

He'd begin his new game tomorrow, he decided, as he searched the night sky for Zeus's constellation, Taurus. The Master needed his help. Okay, he was ready. Minos would exercise his new power; Lucky Red would tell what he knew; the Master would be safe; and the Cretan Bull would dance again. And last but hardly least, Zeus, the cloud gatherer, would smile down on his son.

CHAPTER SEVEN

"It was the Beast, for sure," Sara was saying, after explaining to Abe just why it was a sacrifice to Zeus that the Beast had made in Billy's room. She went over it again—matter of fact—the specifics of how she knew that.

When she finished, Abe said, "I'm sure you're right. It's very impressive how you put that together so quickly—the serpent, the Cretan Bull, Europa, the oak, the thunderbolt..."

It was 10:00 a.m. and Sara and Abe were standing beside the circle she'd drawn in his office. Abe covered the circle with a throw rug when she wasn't there, then uncovered it when she came. She was setting out candles. Abe was lighting them.

"Why Billy?" he asked when she didn't say anything more.

"I'm not sure," she said. "Maybe he's trying to scare *you.*"

"More than anything, he made me mad," Abe said.

"Well you should be scared. He can squeeze the life out of you, easy as squishing a stewed tomato."

Abe made a sour face. "He looked through Billy's things. Lieutenant Ballard thought he was angry when he couldn't find whatever it was that he was looking for."

"Maybe." Sara tried to focus, but clearly had a hard time. "He fucked things up for me with my dad."

"What do you mean?"

"He put a cloud in my mind, made me foggy and stupid."

"How?"

"Dark magic. Zeus's power."

"I'm sorry."

"Something to show you," Sara said. She was wearing old black clothes and she looked gaunt and tired. She turned to Abe who was lighting a candle, and unbuttoned the top two buttons of her blouse. She pulled back her blouse to show him a new tattoo on her chest, just above her breasts. It was a laurel bough. "This might help me," she said, hopeful.

"Laurel?"

"Yes, Apollo's tree."

"That could help." Abe nodded.

After he lit the last candle, Abe turned to Sara, "I've been thinking about Theseus, about his ancestry, and I'd like to go back over your thoughts about his paternity. Please bear with me. Who was Theseus' true father?"

Sara didn't hesitate. "Theseus had two fathers, Aegeus, the king of Athens, and the god, Poseidon—one mortal, one immortal. They were both with his mother, Aethra, on the same night."

"How is that possible?"

"It's not only possible, it makes him a demigod, a divine hero. Greek heroes are said to be demigods if one parent is a god and one is mortal. Sometimes, this scenario is heightened by double paternity. That is to say the seeds of two fathers are mixed in the womb. Hercules' mother carried twins sired on the same night by Zeus and her husband."

"I didn't know that."

"Leda, conceived four children—including Helen of Troy—in the same night by two fathers. Zeus seduced her, in the form of a swan, the other father was her mortal husband."

Abe just sat there, amazed. "How do you know all of this?"

"Silly question." Sara shook her head. "Moira."

"Moira, fate, yes, of course." And Abe knew that that was that. He changed the subject. "You look tired. Are you sleeping?"

"Hardly at all. The Beast is coming after me and my friends in my dreams, turning them to horrible nightmares."

"What does he look like in your dreams?"

"He takes many forms. He comes as the hellhound, or as a lion man, or Pan the Satyr or even the Minotaur. I know it's the Beast because of his weird nightmare smell."

"What's the smell?

"I'm not sure. It's kind of minty." She pursed her lips, closed her eyes. "Can we stop talking about this? It's not helping and it's scaring me." As she said this, Sara wrapped her arms around herself.

"Of course, what would you like to talk about?"

Sara ignored his question. She stepped inside her magic circle. Abe followed, sitting down cross-legged. She was losing focus, chanting softly. Sara began chanting louder. It brought some color to her cheeks.

They had a routine now, she was the Pythia and Abe was the chronicler, a high priest who sat at her feet and wrote down whatever she said, once she was in her trance.

As she chanted, Sara's face turned red. She was swaying back and forth; her hands were raised high above her head. Soon she went into a trance-like state. And after a moment, she cried out, "Satyrs and Maenads—raving followers of Dionysius, divine half-brother of Apollo, with snakes in their hair for Zeus—Maenads in a frenzy, on the rampage, tearing apart their enemies."

Abe wrote in his notebook. "Why?" he asked.

"Murder. Betrayal. Deceit. Punishment." Sara swayed, eyes unfocused, as if possessed. "Pan the Satyr, the goat man, is the chosen lover of the Maenads in their drunken orgies."

"Why?"

"Beware Pan."

"Why Pan?"

"Beware Pan," she prophesied again, gasping for breath, then, almost a whisper, "the goat-devil who hides his hairy black goatishness with well-washed white fleeces." Sara sank to the floor, breathing heavily, red-faced and exhausted.

"Are you OK?" Abe asked, concerned.

She raised her head, then, after a slow, calming breath, she whispered, "…OK?" and shot him a withering look.

◆◆◆

Corey was with Johnny Boy (JB). He'd found Snapper's squat, the abandoned one-room apartment where he'd stayed in Seattle, and taken her there. It was in an older building, scheduled for demolition. There was a table, an old couch with a blanket on it, a cot and an old refrigerator. "He stayed here for three nights," JB explained. "I talked with the street kid who let him use it. Eight Ball, that's the kid's street name, didn't know Snapper, but they had a mutual friend who set this up. Snapper paid the guy a couple bucks a night to stay here. When Snapper died, the other kid split."

Corey took in the old room. She saw a picture, pinned to the wall beside the kitchen sink. She recognized Rawley, Snapper's father. Under the table she saw a laundry bag. In it, there were some clothes and a book. She took out the book, *The Bull from the Sea* by Mary Renault. She could see on the back that it told the story of Theseus, King of Athens. She read, "It opens with his triumphant return from Crete after slaying the Minotaur to mount the throne left empty by the death of his father, Aegeus..."

Corey opened the book In the front of the book, there was an inscription, To Snapper, love, Peter. She wondered who Peter was.

She turned to JB. "Thanks for taking me here. I think Rosa, Snapper's mother, will want this book. And she'll be happy to know that Snapper put up that photo of his dad." Corey took the photo off the wall, put it in the book, then she put the book back in the laundry bag."

"It's the least I could do. Anything else you need here?" JB asked.

When Corey shook her head no, he opened the door. "The Save The Date goes out this week. July seventeenth is the big day."

"It's already in the calendar."

♦♦♦

Minos was in his lab, going through photographs in a scrapbook that he'd opened up on his worktable. It was noon, and the mid day sun illuminated the detail in his painstakingly chosen, carefully organized collection. He'd gathered images of the Minotaur including: William Blake's fantastical drawing to illustrate Inferno XII where Dante and his guide Virgil prepare to enter the Seventh Circle of Hell; Theseus fighting the Minotaur, a marvelous marble statue from 1826 in the Tuileries Gardens, Paris; The

Minotaur in the Labyrinth, a sixteenth century engraving in the Medici Collection in the Palazzo Strozzi, Florence, and so on.

He understood why King Minos hid this monstrous creature in his labyrinth. He'd collected fourteen distinct artist renderings, interpretations, of the cruel and deviate beast, the unnatural offspring of the Cretan Bull and Minos' wife, Pasiphae.

Minos turned to the scholarly articles he kept at the back of his scrapbook. He turned to an historical explanation of the myth. He read how during Minos' reign as King of Crete, tribute from continental Greek cities included young men and women for sacrifice. The ceremony was performed by a priest disguised with a bullhead or mask, thus explaining the imagery of the Minotaur.

One scholar considered it likely that in Crete (where a bull cult may have existed), "Victims were tortured by being shut up in the belly of a red-hot brazen bull."

Minos liked that: a red-hot brazen bull for a red-hot brazen boy.

He had an even better plan, though, for his red-hot brazen boy.

◆◆◆

Doctor Jim Peterson sat at his desk. He was reading a lab report, and tapping the fingers of his left hand on his thigh when the phone rang. He picked it up. "Send him in," was all he said.

A moment later Randy walked into his office, wearing jeans, a tee shirt, and a sport coat clearly chosen for the occasion. "Thanks for seeing me on such short notice, Dr. Peterson," Randy said. "I was able to sign out at three o'clock today, and I came right over."

Jim smiled. He liked Randy, especially his openness. "Thanks for coming by, Randy. If it's about Sara, I'll always find time."

"I called because I'd like to help. I think she's feeling pretty bad."

"You're right about that. Since Snapper died, Sara's gotten worse. She's more and more depressed. It's like his death confirmed all of her fears about what she calls *the Beast*." Jim's face turned weary and sad.

Randy frowned. "I wish there was something more that we could do for her. I mean we really like her, and I hate to see her so low."

"Thank you for that. I'm hoping her therapist can help her, but so far, I'm not seeing much progress. She asked to talk with Peter. I'm thinking that if I can get her in touch with him, maybe he could help."

"That's what I wanted to ask you about. I was hoping that if we could take her to see Peter, or bring Peter back, or even arrange a phone call, that he might be good for her. At least she thinks he'll understand what she's saying. Does that make sense?"

"Yes, it's a very good idea. Sara already suggested it. Peter should be calling in this week—though as you know, he's not always reliable—and when he calls, I'm going to work out a call with Sara." Peter, he knew, would do whatever he could for his sister. "We'll see where we go from there."

"Good. Really good." Randy frowned, pensively.

Jim watched him, aware he was struggling with something. "Is there something else on your mind?"

Randy nodded, making a decision. "Yes, I'd like to talk with you about one other thing."

"Of course."

"For what it's worth, I don't think Snapper's death was an accident or a suicide. I actually agree with Sara—I think Snapper was murdered."

"That's upsetting, and—well—it makes Sara's preoccupations even more unsettling. What makes you say that?"

"Snapper wasn't a druggie, and the Snapper I knew was anything but suicidal. And the makeup—that's not Snapper." Randy frowned. "I thought about going to the police, but in my experience, the police don't listen too well to an eighteen-year-old gay kid with long red hair."

Jim nodded; he got that. "Why don't I go with you to talk with them?" Jim paused, thinking this through. "I think that anything we find out could be helpful. It would be good for Sara to know just what happened. I'd like to see her come to some kind of resolution. Whatever that might be. She has to move on. In her mind, I'm afraid that she's blaming herself for not stopping this monster she calls, *the Beast*. She's being awfully, even dangerously, hard on herself." And it was getting worse. Jim sensed that this self-inflicted guilt was tormenting her.

"That's what she says."

"I have to be at the hospital at four o'clock today. Let's go see the officer in charge after school tomorrow."

"That would be good. I can go anytime after school."

Jim checked his watch. "I have a call with Sara's therapist in just a few minutes. Can we continue this later when we check in with the police? I'll call and see who's handling the case. I can meet you at the station, say four-thirty tomorrow afternoon."

"Perfect. Thanks."

"No. Thank you. I'm grateful that Sara and Peter have such a good friend."

The phone rang as Randy was leaving. "Put him through," Jim said.

"Good to hear from you, Abe."

◆◆◆

Abe sat at his desk, "What can I do for you, Jim?"

"I was just talking with Randy, a friend of Sara's and of Billy's. Everyone's concerned that Sara's getting worse."

"I'm not in that camp."

"Abe, Sara is so scared that she's locking herself in her room at night. She's wandering the street chanting during the day. They won't let her go back to school. When I try and talk with her, she gets angry with me."

"I understand your concerns." And he did, more than Jim knew.

"When can she go back to school? She needs some kind of structure."

"I agree that it would be good for Sara to be in school, but so far they're not ready to readmit her. Maybe we could go and talk with Owen together?"

"Sure, if that would be helpful." Jim paused.

Abe waited, unsure where this was going.

Jim cleared his throat, sucked on his inhaler. "I do have one idea," he eventually offered. "I'd like to get her together with Peter, her half brother, at least on the phone. They've been close since childhood, and she could always talk with him."

"That's a very good idea." He nodded, relieved. "Where is he?"

"Somewhere in the Greek Islands. He shares her love of Greek mythology."

"Could you tell me a little bit more about Peter? Owen said he's an important person for Sara."

"Yes. When we lost Niki, Sara's mother, they became very close. We were vacationing in Greece, where Niki had family, when we discovered that she had cancer. We moved to London, where I put her in a hospital with some of the best cancer doctors in the world. We were too late. Peter was ten, Sara was six. That's when they immersed themselves in Greek mythology. It was the children's way of coping with their terrible loss. Niki introduced them to the myths, then, after she died, Peter would read the myths to Sara day and night. Those were difficult times." Jim paused, reflecting, then changed the subject. "Peter left home last summer. He's taking a year off, traveling."

"Yes, Owen told me that. Is there a particular reason?"

"Frankly, Peter wanted time alone. He's adventurous and rebellious. He's also very bright and capable, so I wasn't worried. Since he was a child, Peter could manage most situations. After talking it through with him, I understood how important this was for him, so I supported his decision. He called last week before he left for the islands. He has no set itinerary, but when he calls in later this week, I'm going to arrange for him to talk with Sara. I'll fly her to Athens if that will help."

"Please don't do that. I'm hopeful that we're making progress working together. Please be patient, and don't interrupt her treatment. A phone call, or bringing him back, could be helpful."

"OK, I'll start by organizing a phone call, but truthfully I'm not feeling at all patient. I'm just not seeing any progress. Have you considered medicating her?"

"Of course I have, but I don't think Sara needs medication. My work with Sara will take time, and it may seem unconventional, but I believe we're making progress. I'd appreciate your patience and your support."

"Abe, I sincerely hope you know what you're doing, but if I don't see positive developments soon, I'm going to consider other options. My daughter is suffering. She's lost in this dark, crazy world she's created in her mind. That world is growing more intense, more real, every day...I'm not sure that she shouldn't be hospitalized."

Abe scowled, aware that Jim was putting him on notice; he was running out of time. "I appreciate your concerns, Jim. Please bear with us. Let's schedule a time to see Owen together."

"Yes, fine. Please remember what I've said."

"Of course. Goodbye, Jim." Abe hung up the phone, aware that this was likely to get harder before it became even a little bit easier. He hoped Jim would give him time. He had to genuinely understand Sara's world—not just abstractly, but empathically, even viscerally—then connect with her in it. He couldn't do that yet. They were, however, making progress. He was, somehow, sure of that.

◆◆◆

Minos could see them all through the window of the café—the gaggle of youngsters that somehow held the key to solving his problem. They were at their table in the back. He could count on finding them there every day after school. He was in his car today, because he'd need it later. He'd dressed for the occasion—black cashmere sweater, grey herringbone sport coat, black dress slacks, classic, brushed-suede hush puppies, even a handkerchief in his breast pocket. Though he still had a faint scar, it was not as noticeable now, and his makeup was generally lighter. There was no purple birthmark.

Today, he sported curly black hair, a beard and a neatly trimmed mustache. Professorial was the look he was after. Checking in the rear view mirror, he thought he saw a twinkle in his eye through his wire-rimmed glasses. When Lucky Red got up and went out onto the street, Minos followed.

Ten minutes later Lucky Red stopped at a coffee shop on Broadway, and Minos found a parking place nearby. Minos followed him into the coffee shop, carrying a tan leather briefcase. He approached his table. At the table he smiled then said, "You must be Randy. My name is Francis, Professor Francis Duncan. I'm faculty, here at the U. I have a message for you from your friend, Peter."

"How did you know who I was?"

"Peter said to look for the handsome fellow with the long red hair at the Blue City Café after school. You fit the bill. I drove up as you were leaving and followed you here in my car." Minos pointed out a blue Dodge, parked down the street. This is a very sweet game, he was thinking.

Randy looked at him, still confused. "How do you know Peter?"

"We spent time together in London last week. I'm an art historian, and I was a visiting lecturer at the British Museum. He approached me after my lecture on the Elgin Marbles. When I told him I was faculty at the University of Washington, we struck up a conversation. We hit it off right away. He's a very bright and charming young man. I was most impressed with his knowledge of Greek mythology. Not my field really, but related…" From his briefcase, Minos took a street artist's rendering of Peter sitting on the steps in front of the British Museum. He set the drawing on the table. "I drew this last week. He looks good, doesn't he? He wanted you to have it." And his plan was working, he could tell. It helped that Randy wasn't too smart or too careful, and that he so wanted to hear about Peter. This was, he decided, a very cool game. Yeah.

Randy nodded, pleased. "Yeah, he looks great."

"He sends his best to you, and he asked you to tell Sara that he sent her a postcard. I also have a drawing for Sara." Francis took out a sketch of Peter looking up at two marble metopes from the Parthenon—human Lapiths battling Centaurs, part man, part horse. The mythical battle depicted on the metopes were part of the Elgin Marbles taken from the Parthenon to the British Museum. "When I left, he was on his way to Crete."

"She'll be happy to hear that. And even happier to get your sketch."

Francis handed it to Randy. "Will you give it to her?"

"Of course. She'll be thrilled." He pulled out a chair for Francis then turned back to his rendering of Peter. "You're talented—a professor and an artist."

"You're very kind. I study, teach, and write about art history—hence my interest in the Marbles. The drawing is more of a hobby."

Randy looked again at the picture of Peter in London. "I'd like to get in touch with him. It's important. Do you have a way to contact him?"

There it was. Minos sprung his trap. "Yes, as a matter of fact, I think I can help with that. He's staying with a friend of mine in Crete. He checked his watch. With the time change, we ought to be able to reach them at my friend, Minos' house now." It was a cheap shot, but he couldn't resist. "If you'd like, we can stop by my office here on Capitol Hill and make the call right away."

Randy checked his watch. "I have to meet someone at six o'clock, here on the Hill. That gives us over an hour. Is that enough time?"

"No problem. Hop in the car and we'll be at the office in five minutes. After you talk with your friend, I'll drop you off for your meeting."

"I'm excited. Francis, thank you." He shook Minos' hand.

Minos smiled. "My pleasure, young fellow. Peter will be surprised and delighted." Minos opened the car door and Randy stepped in.

Gotcha, Lucky Red.

◆◆◆

Sara was walking down Pike, going west, past Broadway. It was four-thirty, and the street was lively. Her bag was slung over her shoulder. With her spiked collar, her red streaked hair and her blouse unbuttoned to show off her new tattoo, she fit right in. She was chanting, trying to turn off her mind. The Beast was out this evening, stronger than ever, readying to kill again, Sara was sure of that. But she didn't know what to do. No one was helping her. Not the gods, not her dad, not her shrink. The bear shrink was trying—at least he seemed to believe her—but trying wasn't the same as helping. She felt hopeless, and her mind was racing like a runaway train.

She peered into a coffee shop window, hoping to see someone she knew, anything to distract her, but she didn't recognize anyone, so she kept chanting. She checked out a tattoo parlor. In the front window, they featured S&M photos—a leather-clad dominatrix whipping a hand-cuffed man, men punishing women, women flogging other women, threesomes, every imaginable combination. It made her think of the furies taking their horrible vengeance with their brass-studded scourges. Sara made a grim face. This was scaring her.

On the street, someone called her name. It was Sean, an old friend of Peter's from middle school. He used to hang out at their house. Sean was a senior at Olympic, and even though he sometimes hung with the popular crowd, he was always nice to her whenever they crossed paths in the halls. He was driving and he waved her over. Sara got in his car, glad to have a distraction.

"Hey Sara, I heard about what happened at school. Sorry."

"Let's not talk about it. I'm still really bummed," she explained.

"OK. You wanna hang out?"

"Yeah. Sure." Sara nodded relieved. Her mind was still racing. She started chanting, a low murmur.

Sean looked over at her. "You okay?"

"I'm scared. And I'm wound too tight. It's like I'm speeding…in my mind."

"I've got just the thing." He touched Sara's arm. "You wanna try some ecstasy?" Sean asked. "It's good shit in a small dose. Take the edge right off."

"Yeah. That would be good," Sara said, like she knew what it was. She didn't even know where those words came from, but she felt better already.

Sean drove to Olympic, where they parked in the school's empty parking lot. He took a small plastic bag from the glove compartment, took two pills out, and gave one to Sara.

He passed her a water bottle. Sara took the pill.

"Tilt your seat back," Sean suggested. "Lay back and close your eyes. It won't take long." Sean tilted his own seat back, reclining into it.

Sara wasn't sure how much time had passed before she began to feel better—sort of a warm, soft glow. When she felt Sean's hand on her breast it felt good, and she responded tenderly when he kissed her lips. Yeah, this was way better than being afraid all of the time.

Sometime later, she wasn't sure how long, he spread her legs with his hand. When he unzipped his pants she whispered, "No. No…"

Maybe he didn't hear her, because she felt his finger inside her. She pushed him away. "I don't want that," she explained.

"Your first time?" Sean asked. "You're going to love it." He took out a condom.

Sara watched him put the condom on, take her panties off, and kneel between her legs. This wasn't happening to her, she was thinking. This was someone else and she was watching. She wasn't sure just what she was watching but it hurt when he started to push inside her.

Sara screamed, "NO!" and pushed him away as hard as she could. He rolled off of her. She opened the door, grabbed her bag and ran from the car. She was crying now and running as fast as she could.

Sometime later, she wasn't sure how long, she circled back to the bench outside the school. She sat there, crying softly. Even though she was high, her mind was racing again. Sara kept seeing the Furies—snakes for hair, coal-black bodies, blood dripping from their eyes. Zeus's father, the Titan, Cronus, had castrated his own father, Uranus, and thrown his genitals into the sea. The Furies had risen from the drops of Uranus' blood that fell on the earth. She saw them now—hideous fiends, born from the blood, created to punish. They carried brass-studded scourges, and their victims died in torment. Sara closed her eyes, lowered her head and wrapped her arms around each other.

Sometime later, she took her cell phone from her bag, dialed Dr. Stein's number. When she recognized Abe's deep voice, she whispered, "Help me, please." Then she started crying again.

"Where are you, Sara?"

"On the bench, in front of my school."

"I'll be there right away."

A few minutes later the burgundy Olds with the neat white trim pulled up in front of the bench. Abe stepped hurriedly out of the passenger door. Sam, his driver, was at the wheel.

Abe sat on the bench next to Sara. She was still crying. "What happened Sara?"

She took a calming breath. "The Beast clouded my mind. I took ecstasy, then Peter's friend, Sean, tried to have me, to ravish me, like Zeus.

I had to push him off. Right there." She pointed to the parking lot. The car was gone. "I'm sorry. I'm still high, and my mind is racing. I keep seeing the Furies, inflicting their terrible vengeance, and it scares me."

"It's not your fault. The Furies aren't going to hurt you. I promise you that. Do you need a doctor?"

"No, it hurt, but I didn't let him really do it. My mind is messed up, but physically, I'm okay."

"Did he force you?"

"Sort of, but not really. At the beginning, I said yes, then I was like watching. I dunno."

"Do you want to go to the police?"

"No. No. It was a trick, a distraction. I need to stop the Beast. He's risen. I need to stop him before he kills again." And she just knew this—in her gut, in her bones.

"Why?"

"Peirithous is in danger." She had to reach Theseus. Right away.

"Who's Peirithous?"

Sara made a sour face, impatient. "Agh! You already know that. I told you that. Theseus' best friend." She began chanting, softly.

"Yes, alright… Can I take you home, Sara? Would you like to get some rest?"

She took a slow breath. "No. And please don't tell my dad."

"If this was date rape, he should know about it."

"It was the Beast fucking up my mind. I may be high but I know what happened… It's not what you think… I went in the car. I took the drugs. I liked it when he touched me, kissed me. I just watched when he tried to push inside me, then, when it hurt, I pushed him off. And *I don't want to talk about it anymore*, especially with my father. My dad thinks I'm crazy, out of control. Don't make it worse for me. Please."

"Why don't we ask him to come in with you tomorrow morning. We can talk with him together. I'll help you. And Sara, you're not crazy."

"Thanks for that." He was nice. If only he could help.

"You're welcome. Sara, for now, I just want to be sure that you're alright, then we can decide what you'd like to do."

"More talking?" He didn't really get that someone was about to die. If she told him again, he'd want to talk about it. Shit.

"Reassure me."

"Right here, on the bench?"

"Here. At the office…at your house…wherever you'd like."

"You're sapping my strength. *The Beast* has Risen." Sara knew then, just what she had to do. To do it, she had to ditch this guy. There was no other way. She collected herself, speaking carefully. "OK, yes, I'll take your advice. Take me home. I could use some down time. And don't worry, I'm OK. Yeah, I'm OK. Could we talk about everything in the morning? Everything. My dad, too."

"Are you sure?"

"Yes. I'm sure. Tomorrow morning, with my dad. I'll take it easy tonight, think about what I want to say tomorrow."

Abe took out one of his business cards. On the back he wrote down his cell phone number. He gave it to Sara. "You can reach me at this number anytime. Please call me if you need help."

"Thank you."

"Now, please call your father. Make sure he's home to take care of you."

Sara dialed the number. "Dad I'm on my way home. Will you be there?"

"Yes, of course. Is everything OK?" her father asked her.

"The usual—the Beast is making it hard for me, I'll see you soon."

"Done," Sara said to Abe, then getting up to go, "Who's driving?" she asked, nodding at Sam.

"That's Sam, my driver. I don't drive."

Sara put on her game face. "I bet that's a story and a half."

Abe chuckled. "It is. Long story short, I get distracted and I sideswipe parked cars. The judge won't let me drive."

"You're worse off than I am. I mean you set fires in your office, you drop tobacco and ashes from your pipe all over your desk, you sideswipe parked cars. C'mon, how can you help me fight the Beast if you're always distracted?" She watched him, considering her question. Shit, he thought about everything. She felt bad about ditching the guy, but she had no choice. None.

"Sara—"

His deep voice, so serious, brought her back.

"I can't drive because I'm so relentlessly focused on whatever it is I'm thinking about. Right now, I'm focused on helping you find Theseus. You understand that. I'm sure you lose track of time and forget practical things when you're going into your trance as the Pythia, trying to channel Apollo."

"Yeah, I do…" And thinking about that, "Shit, I don't have my panties."

◆◆◆

As soon as Abe's driver dropped her off, Sara began working on her dad. "Hey, Dad, will you come with me to see Dr. Stein tomorrow morning?"

"Is that alright with him?"

"Yeah, it was his idea. There's stuff the three of us should talk about."

"That could be helpful. I'd like to know how it's going, how I can help."

"I think it's time."

"You seem to be feeling better."

"Yeah, I am. Some of the kids are going to the film club at school tonight. They're showing that old movie, *The Graduate*. Is it okay if I go? Alex is driving. He'll pick me up."

"Yes, that's a good idea. I'm glad you're going out with friends, feeling better."

"Let me go get ready," Sara said, thinking her plan was working. She still felt the drug, but she was coming down. Her plan was anchoring her.

She went upstairs, called Alex. He agreed to pick her up in ten minutes. She gathered all of the things she needed in a black gym bag and in her shoulder bag. At the bottom of her shoulder bag she checked to be sure she had her sacrifice—a quarter pound of meat cut from a lamb shank. It was a compromise—she'd asked for bull meat—but she thought it would work. The butcher had wrapped it in white butcher paper. She remembered his creepy, dirty-old-man look after she rejected his suggestion of Rocky Mountain Oysters.

After she gathered everything she would need, Sara picked up her gym bag with her left hand, slung her canvas bag over her right shoulder, called out her goodbye to her dad, who was reading in the living room, and went outside to wait for Alex. Her mind was steady now. She was already focused on what she had to do.

CHAPTER EIGHT

Once a month, Abe and Corey invited Abe's mother, Jesse Stein, to dinner. Tonight, they'd also included their friend, Lieutenant Lou Ballard, Jason Weiss—Jesse's lawyer and a lifelong friend of Abe and Abe's father—and of course, Billy, who viewed these dinners as, at best, a way to use his grandmother's influence to get good seats to a Mariners or a Seahawks game. Twice in the past year, he'd scored tickets to big-time rock concerts.

Corey didn't care for her mother-in-law, the only person in the world who regularly made her feel inadequate. No one could get under her skin like Jesse.

"What exactly is it that you do?" Jesse asked Corey, raising a longstanding prickly issue between them. "That is to say, what is your actual profession?"

Corey went on automatic pilot. Last year, Jesse had tried to buy her a travel agency so she'd have a *real job*. "As you know, I find runaways. Once found, they become the client, and I help them sort out what to do."

"Who pays for this?"

"Usually a parent or a grandparent."

"Isn't it frustrating? I mean, most of these young people don't bathe."

Jason looked out the window.

Abe shot Corey a please-don't-kill-her look.

"Excuse me," Corey said, standing up. "I have to check on something in the kitchen." She went out through the kitchen door.

Jesse turned to Lou. "You're a policeman, do you understand what it is my daughter-in-law does?"

"Actually, I do, and she does it extremely well."

"Give me an example."

"Whenever I need to find a young person who's living off the radar, and that sometimes happens when they've seen something, or seen someone that we need to talk to, I go to Corey. She grumbles about how she doesn't do police work, but if I need her, I know I can count on her. The kids trust her and they help her. She's earned that. They often don't trust police officers."

"Yes," Jason agreed. "Corey's also helped me locate missing young people."

"Wasn't one of these young people found dead not long ago in Volunteer Park?" Jesse queried. And, an afterthought, "That's near my neighborhood."

Abe put a hand on his mother's arm. "Please, let's change the subject. The young man they found was one of Corey's clients."

"Why is it that I'm not surprised?" Then, after a beat: "Why didn't I know this?"

"Mom, it's private."

"Psychiatrists and lawyers, their interactions with their clients are protected by confidentiality. I get that." Jesse glared at her son—she was unsheathing her skinning knife. "But I guarantee you that confidentiality doesn't extend to unlicensed, runaway hunters."

Abe frowned his disapproval then changed the subject. "Lou, did you find anything more on cause of death for Snapper—Bud Parker?"

"Not yet. I leaned on them pretty hard to run every possible poison."

"Ask them to test for the alkaloid pseudaconitine, a deadly poison found in the plant Aconitum, also known as wolfsbane. I did some research." Abe handed Lou a piece of paper. On it, he'd scribbled the specifics on the poison. "Twenty milliliters will kill an adult human."

"They put it on darts in *Game of Thrones*," Billy added. "Very strong stuff."

Corey came back from the kitchen, carrying a tray of vegetables.

Abe smiled at her. "Lou's going to check Snapper for wolfsbane. In Greek mythology, Medea tries to poison Theseus by putting it in his wine."

"Is Snapper the street person they found dead—made up to look like a battered old man in Volunteer Park?" Jesse asked.

"Right."

"And you, my son, and his wife…" Jesse glanced at Corey. "…the unlicensed, runaway hunter, are saying he's part of some Greek myth."

Instead of upending the vegetables in Jesse's lap, Corey set them down, smiled and asked, "Why Jesse, wasn't your old boyfriend, Nick Season, Greek? As I remember, he was right out of Greek mythology—cursed to tell treacherous lies, doomed to manipulate, seduce and deceive powerful, older women."

Jason closed his eyes, readying himself.

Jesse's face turned red. She turned to Abe. "How is it possible, even conceivable, that you, this woman's husband, are the fruit of my loins?"

"Indeed." Corey said.

Abe nodded, gravely. "A conundrum."

Jason tugged at his earlobe with a thumb and forefinger. A tell Abe recognized.

Straight-faced, Jason offered, "An old Jewish saying that is, perhaps, applicable." He nodded, tapping a thumb and forefinger in the air, for emphasis. "In the old country it was said, 'Life's great mysteries, in the end, they are often inexplicable.'"

For a moment there was total silence and baffled expressions, then Abe gave Jason a thumbs up. "…Voilà! Bravo!" he exclaimed. Jason, an expert mediator, had a knack for diffusing awkward situations. He was a student of the nonsensical cliché.

Billy joined in, serious-faced. "Of course…yes…sometimes you eat the bear…and sometimes the bear eats you."

Corey laughed out loud. She loved these guys.

Jesse forced an icy smile.

Lou looked away. Corey thought he was blushing.

◆◆◆

Sara was in the woods, at her spot. Alex had dropped her off at the Italian intersection, and she'd walked in from there. A potion was brewing in her little cauldron. The cauldron sat on a tripod above a propane flame, and her potion was bubbling inside the iron bowl. She'd drawn her circle around the cauldron. Her candles were lit at the edge of the circle. In the circle, Sara had set an olive branch, a lamb bone, various totems she'd collected, even some Theseus memorabilia. She added olive oil, wine, herbs, and rock salt to her potion. When she was satisfied, Sara drank from her vial of wine, honey, chopped cheese and meal—her homemade ambrosia.

With her Athame, Sara cut off a piece of meat from the lamb shank. She lowered it into her cauldron. "I sacrifice this baby lamb to you great Apollo, god of truth and prophecy." Sara raised her Athame above her head. Softly she whispered, "I am the priestess, the vestal virgin, secret sister of Theseus. I pray to Apollo, who slayed Python, the serpent, at Delphi. I must find Theseus. I need him now. I call on Apollo to help me find him. I need him now..." She drank her homemade ambrosia as she called, "Blue-haired Poseidon, master of ships and stallions, you who sired him, lead me to Theseus. I call on Theseus. The Beast is rising. I need him now..." As she chanted, Sara swayed, her Athame held high.

She stepped closer to the cauldron, chewing a laurel leaf now, as the Pythia did at Delphi, to help induce a trance. She swayed back and forth, eyes on the boiling potion, then cried out, "Nothing. You grant me nothing. Then there must be blood. The gods must dance in blood." Sara stiffened, then she brought her Athame down, slicing across her forearm. "Accept my offering, great Apollo, keeper of light. And to you, Poseidon, breaker of ships and cities, I offer again to you, to appease your anger." Sara sliced again, letting her blood flow down her elbow and into the bubbling cauldron. "Take me. I am your vessel. Let me cry out your prophecy."

As she swayed and chanted, her face turned red. Beads of sweat appeared on her brow, she made guttural noises, and then she began to shake, finally possessed. When she spoke, her voice was harsh. It wasn't Apollo, nor Poseidon, who prophesied. No, it was Pasiphae, Minos' wife, who cursed Minos for his many infidelities, who spoke through Sara's mouth, "Why have the furies not punished you?" Sara, the Pythoness, cried out. "You, a mere mortal who taunts the Cretan Bull. By my curse, it is you, brazen child, who will dance in blood." Twirling now, Sara slashed her arm yet gain. This time, her knife cut much deeper, and her blood spewed across the clearing. Sara screamed and ran from her spot, through the woods and out onto the road.

A car was leaving the Hebrew Academy parking lot, and the driver stopped when he saw the blood-drenched girl, lying in a fetal ball on the road. He dialed 911. "We need an ambulance, right away. It's a life-threatening emergency…"

The driver had a first aid kit and was able to bandage her arm and slow the bleeding. Sara was still alive when the paramedics arrived.

◆◆◆

Minos was looking down at Randy, who was tied down to a cot in his lab. It was the same gurney that had hosted Snapper. There was a canvas strap across Randy's chest. His wrists and his ankles were tied to the cot's metal frame, and his mouth was taped shut. Randy had been sedated, and he was asleep.

Minos was no longer disguised as Francis, the professor. He wore black pants and a black turtleneck. His makeup was heavier. The scar that ran over his left eye, leaving it partially closed, then up across his forehead, was thicker and more prominent. His purple birthmark spread boldly, like a dark stain across his cheek. His brow was also scarred, purposefully.

As he waited, Minos lifted Randy's mobile phone from where he'd left it on his makeup table. He scrolled through his text messages back and forth with Alex—there were hundreds of them. When he found what he was looking for, Minos sent a text of his own, liking this new game.

Minos set the phone down, then stood in front of his mirror. He took a minute, stretching, loosening up. When he felt silky inside, Minos danced his own version of a Cretan Bull dance, part pantomime, part shadow boxing, part Crane dance. The Crane dance featured turnings and windings, and was said to be an imitation of the windings of the Cretan Labyrinth. Legend had it that Theseus first performed this dance in Delos, on his return from Crete after escaping from the labyrinth. Minos twisted and turned, then his hands found their marks in the air, fingers curling up like horns beside his head.

When he'd finished dancing, Minos watched Randy wake up. He loved the terrified look in his eyes, the way he tried, unsuccessfully, to free his bound hands and feet, and, best of all, the muffled screams that came from underneath the duct tape.

◆◆◆

"She's always been like that," Abe said to Corey. "Impossibly intrusive. Asking inappropriate questions, ignoring boundaries, flaunting her status. She actually judges, then ranks, people in her own carefully constructed hierarchy of prestige and influence. That's why she's so negative about what you do—it doesn't score well in her system."

"It will always be a mystery to me that she's so successful," Corey said.

"As good as she is at getting under your skin, she's even better at ingratiating herself to powerful people and then leveraging that power. She's very smart, and she has an eye for the jugular."

"She's always looking for my weak spot," Billy added. He shrugged. "She can be nice when she wants to. I mean she's way nicer to me than she is to you, mom. And dad's right, when she wants you to like her, she takes care of business, like football tickets. Even though she hates football and thinks it's barbaric, like gladiators."

Abe's phone rang. He looked at the number and picked up immediately. "I'm on my way," was all he said.

He called Sam, who had a room over their garage, and asked him to meet him at the car. Normally, Sam would have complained about his lot in life, driving this crazy psychiatrist around at all hours of the night, but Abe's tone ruled that out.

He turned back to Corey and Billy, "I have to go to the hospital. Sara had an accident. They said her condition was stable. She had my card with her. I'll call her dad from the car. Honey, will you call Lou, ask him to meet me there. I have a bad feeling about this. I'll call you guys when I know more." And then he was out the door.

◆◆◆

At the hospital, the emergency room doctor explained to Abe that Sara had lost a lot of blood, but she was going to be okay. She was sleeping now. She had three cuts, one of them quite deep, on her left forearm. They had no idea what had happened, who had inflicted her wounds.

"Did she have a shoulder bag or a duffle bag with her when the ambulance came?"

"No, she was lying in the road, covered with blood. No possessions. The police found both bags later, in the woods."

"Can I see her?" Abe asked. "I'm her therapist. I think I can explain what happened."

"She's in room one-forty-one. Go down this hall, then hang a right." The emergency room doctor pointed out the direction. "Let yourself in. She's sedated."

"Thank you, I'll find you before I leave."

Lou Ballard was waiting for Abe in front of Sara's room when he arrived. "Jesus, doc, trouble sticks to you like a friggin' tar baby," he said by way of greeting. "Your patient started a fire in Interlaken Park. She had some kind of Voodoo potion brewing in an iron cauldron. And we found her blood-stained, double-bladed dagger on the ground nearby. There were candles all over the place. She must of knocked one of them over when she ran out to the street. The only reason we found it at all was because the paramedics saw smoke pluming from the woods."

"I can explain. Please don't charge her. Just leave her in my care, and I'll be responsible for her."

"And why should I do that?"

"She believes someone else is about to die. She was right about Bud Parker. If you let me continue to work with her, I think we may be able to help you solve the murder."

"What murder? We have no evidence. And yes, we're testing for your ancient poison. But it's not something they've ever done. The ME I work with isn't exactly a classical Greek scholar. Incidentally, he wanted to know who's the joker named a poison after a band."

Abe smiled. "Lou, in spite of tonight, I feel like Sara and I are close to a breakthrough."

"Breakthrough?" Lou cracked his knuckles. "Remind me never to send anyone to you for help."

"I need to see her, then I'll explain what I can." Abe opened her door. Lou took a seat in the hallway.

In her room, Abe watched Sara. She was sleeping peacefully. He knew she didn't get much peaceful sleep. He checked her pulse, then her bandages. Yes, it was possible that she'd used her Athame to make a blood sacrifice in her efforts to reach Apollo. He decided to let her sleep. He'd talk with her later.

When he stepped out of Sara's room, Abe saw Jim Peterson, racing down the hall, inhaler blasting. "Jim," he put a hand on Jim's shoulder when he arrived. "She's fine, sedated and sleeping peacefully. Let's find a place where we can talk. I'd like to ask Lieutenant Ballard to join us." Abe nodded toward the pear-shaped lieutenant with the thin tie seated in the hallway.

"Lou, I'd like to introduce Dr. Jim Peterson, Sara's father." Lou stood, extended his hand.

"Jim Peterson." Jim shook Lou's offered hand. "Is this a police matter?"

"I hope not," Lou said, truthfully. "Let's find a place to talk."

"I can arrange that," Jim said, then to Abe, "This happened on your watch. I hope you can explain that."

♦♦♦

"Abe, you're her therapist. You're supposed to make sure that this kind of thing *doesn't happen*," Jim said, plainly upset, after Abe walked them through what he thought had happened in the woods. "And it's just getting worse since she started seeing you. You're encouraging her fantasies, her mythological hocus pocus, her do-it-yourself witchcraft." Jim took a hit on his inhaler. "She could have died tonight from her self-inflicted wounds."

"I understand how you feel, and truthfully, I didn't expect anything like this. But I have a different understanding of what Sara's doing. When I dropped Sara off at your house, earlier this evening, she'd just had a frightening experience with a friend from school. We can talk more about that when she's ready. She ran away and called me. I discussed it with her and she didn't want to talk with you about it yet. She wasn't hurt, and we made a plan to talk with you about everything tomorrow morning, which I'd still like to do."

"You decided to wait? I think that's poor judgment."

"Perhaps, but after everything she'd been through today, I had no idea that she was still so very worried about the Beast killing someone. Can you imagine how intense those feelings had to be that she'd try again to find Theseus tonight? *She had to be certain that lives were at stake.* She lied to both of us—*her father and her therapist*—to get back to her magic circle in the woods. She believes there's a killer out there, and she's taking very real risks to do something about it. Until we talk with her, let's at least give her the benefit of the doubt.

"This is scaring me," Jim explained. "She's blaming herself for her friend Snapper's death. She's teetering on the very edge. I remind you again—those were self-inflicted wounds tonight."

Abe furrowed his bushy brow. He wasn't going there. "Jim, what if Sara's right? What if her friends are in danger?" he asked, ignoring Jim's pained expression. "Lou, I'd like you to try and find all of Sara's friends. That would be Alex, Randy, Billy, and his girlfriend, Amy, and anyone else that Owen, the dean at Olympic, or Jim, thinks we should check on. They all hang out at the Blue City Café."

"You're just validating the same anxious fantasies that led to this near catastrophe."

"What do we have to lose by asking Lou to check it out? If everyone's fine, then that will, at least, reassure Sara. Think of it as a precaution."

"Dr. Peterson, I know Abe pretty well," Lou intervened. "He's unconventional, irritating, and generally off putting, but he's often right. The reason that I'm not pressing charges against your daughter is that she's under his care, and he's agreed to take responsibility for her."

"I appreciate that," Jim offered.

"I'm going to follow up, check on these kids. And Dr. Peterson, if I could offer up some advice—stick with Abe. Even though I get how that's—what's that word?—counterintuitive. Yeah, counterintuitive."

"I do appreciate that you're vouching for him, Lieutenant. You can see that from where I sit, this looks pretty grim. I will go along with this plan." Jim hesitated then added, "Sara's friend, Randy, came to see me today. He was worried about Sara. Before he left, he said he, too, believed that their friend, Snapper, was murdered. I'm supposed to meet him at the police station tomorrow to speak to the person handling the case."

"That's me," Lou said.

"Okay. Good. Is there any evidence that Snapper was murdered?"

"Not yet. We're running some more tests."

"Alright. I'll wait for the lieutenant to check on Sara's friends. But if they're all fine, and if there's no evidence of foul play in Snapper's death, then we're going to revisit other options. And in spite of the lieutenant's kind words about you, Abe, I still need to be convinced that the treatment is working. My daughter almost bled to death while under your care. I need to see her getting better, not getting lost in some weird mix of Greek mythology and black magic. Take care of my daughter, Abe. Please..."

"I'll do my best—you can rely on that...and thanks, Jim, for bearing with me. I'm going to want to talk with Sara when she wakes up, then the three of us should talk tomorrow."

"Yes, what you told me about earlier, I'd like to hear about that."

"I understand, and you will. Let's give Sara a night to regroup. Jim, I think there's an opportunity here. Let's talk with Sara about all of this when she's ready. In the meantime, will you call Owen and ask if there are any other friends of hers we should check on?"

"Yes, of course."

"Lou, please let me know as soon as you know anything."

"I'm on it."

"Jim, have you had any luck reaching Peter?"

"I got a message on my machine at home this morning. He's calling again the day after tomorrow."

"Good. I'd like to talk with him, too."

"I'll set that up."

Lou was already on the phone, sending a police officer to the Blue City Café.

At the Blue City, Billy, Amy, and Alex were at their table in the back. A policeman was at the door. "Sara's going to be OK," Billy said. "My dad called in from the hospital. The police will check in with us regularly until this is sorted out." Billy nodded toward the policeman at the door.

"Why would she cut herself? She must be really sure that something bad is going to happen. I can't get it out of my mind," Alex said. "There's definitely something weird going down—I mean Snapper, the sacrifice thing in your room, Billy, whoever went through my things, police protection for godsake, and now Sara hurting herself…"

"Where's Randy?" Amy asked Alex.

"He texted me. He's away for the weekend with his dad."

"His dad takes him out of school?"

"Yeah. His dad called him in sick today. It's Friday. He sometimes does that and then they go fishing for the long weekend. They don't get that much time together, and his dad really likes to fish. They drive over the mountains and float the Yakima River when they can."

"I agree with Alex," Billy said. "Something is off. I'm going to ask my mom and dad tonight to help us."

"I'd like to be there too," Amy said.

"Alex?"

"Can't. The moms only let me out because they're cooking a special dessert for me. They'll freak out if I'm not there. Please call me after." He checked his watch. "Eighty-thirty. Got to go."

Billy already had his cell phone out. "Mom, can Amy come over tonight? I know it's short notice, but we want to talk about everything that's going down… Thanks… What time will dad be back? Nine-thirty's not too late." Billy nodded yes to Amy who was already on the phone with her mom.

Sara was sitting up in bed. Abe sat in a chair beside her. "Where's Peirithous?" she asked.

"I don't know. I asked Lieutenant Ballard to check on all of your friends. He'll let us know about everyone soon. Can you tell me what happened Sara?"

"I was possessed, only it wasn't Apollo who prophesied. It was Minos' wife, Pasiphae, who spoke through my mouth. She accused me, a mere mortal, of taunting the Cretan Bull. She said that the furies would punish me for that. Then she cursed me—she said that I was a brazen child, and that I would dance in blood." Sara's lips turned up in the trace of a smile. "I'd say her curse worked pretty well."

Abe had to smile. This terrifically bright young woman was so resilient. "Tell me about the Cretan Bull."

"The way I put it together, Zeus first took the form of a snow white bull to abduct Europa, the beautiful, virgin, Phoenician princess. She and her friends were picking flowers when she saw the lovely white bull. She was struck by his beauty, and she stroked his flanks and hung garlands from his horns. When he lay on the grass, she climbed onto his back. She rode the bull to the edge of the sea, whereupon Zeus immediately swam to Crete with Europa on his back. Once there, Zeus revealed his true identity, and Europa became Crete's first queen. Zeus and Europa had three sons. One of them was Minos, who called the Cretan Bull from the sea, years later, as proof of his right to reign in Crete. Later, that same bull sired the Minotaur with Minos' wife, Pasiphae, the same woman who cursed me."

Abe thought about this for a minute. Wheels within wheels. "If you're taunting the Cretan Bull, does that mean the Cretan Bull is the Beast?"

"Toward the end of his life, he could have been. When Zeus first appeared as the Cretan Bull, he was gentle and beautiful. In Cretan legend, he had a silver circle on his brow and horns like the crescent of the young moon. This bull bore no resemblance to the Beast."

"And later?"

"When Poseidon brought him forth from the sea for Minos, he was also tame and beautiful. But when Minos didn't sacrifice him to Poseidon as promised, Poseidon was enraged and struck the bull, making the fine, gentle bull mad and wild. In this state he mated with Pasiphae, fathered the Minotaur and wreaked havoc in Crete. Eventually Theseus captured him in Marathon and took him to Athens where he sacrificed the bull. Theseus then went to Crete where he killed the Minotaur."

"I'm beginning to understand why you'd make a blood sacrifice to find Theseus. At the same time, though, I need you to understand, absolutely, that I can't let you hurt yourself, Sara. I don't want this to happen again."

"I have to find him."

"I get that. But I can't let you hurt yourself."

"I didn't hurt myself, as you put it. I made a blood sacrifice to get Apollo's attention. It didn't work, then Pasiphae, who gave birth to the Minotaur, laid a pretty heavy curse on me. She's one terrifying bitch, too. Think about it—she not only made bestial love with a bull, she cast a spell on her husband, Minos, so that if he made love to another woman he discharged serpents, scorpions and centipedes… Remember that?"

Abe nodded, grave. "It's unforgettable."

"Can you imagine? And this insane immortal bitch is protecting the Beast."

Abe let this sink in. Pasiphae was—as Sara rightly put it—one terrifying bitch. Yet this was coming from somewhere in Sara's own mind. Why, he wondered, was Sara getting cursed by such a formidable adversary? "Sara, is it possible that you're punishing yourself? That on some level you actually want to bleed out?"

"Of course not. Why would I want that?"

"Perhaps because you have some terrible knowledge. That is to say you know something that you hate knowing. A thing that is somehow toxic, poisonous. You could feel like you've been poisoned—that you're somehow toxic on the inside, and you, literally, want to get the bad blood out."

"That's psycho mumbo jumbo. Totally. You have no idea whatsoever what it's like to be cursed, or tormented by the Furies."

"That's true."

"We don't have time for mumbo-jumbo." She spat it out.

"I'm sorry. You're right about that." And she was right, it was a mistake to have said it. His world, not hers.

"The Beast knows that I'm his enemy. Somehow, he has to stop me. He'll use all of his power to do that. So he sent Pasiphae to curse me. She would have killed me if she could have. But even ghastly Pasiphae, Minos' immortal bitch wife, can't stop Moira. That's what saved my life."

"Do I have to worry about this happening again?"

"Of course you do. The closer we get to the Beast, the more he'll do to stop me. But don't you see, this means we're getting closer."

Abe squeezed her hand, thinking that, in her way, she was making more sense than he was. "OK. Fair enough. Though sometimes, it's hard to keep up with you… Sara, I'm going to stay close until we find Theseus."

◆◆◆

When Abe came through their front door and into the living room, Billy, Amy and Corey were in the middle of an intense conversation. Corey turned to him right away. "How's Sara?"

"She's lost some blood, but she'll be okay." Abe sat beside Corey on the couch, took her hand in his big palm. He was facing Amy and Billy. He extended his other hand to Amy, who shook it firmly. "Glad you're here, Amy," Abe offered. "Sorry about the circumstances."

She nodded. "Good to be here, especially under the circumstances."

Abe nodded back; he liked her already.

The phone rang. Corey picked it up. "Yes, they're right here in our living room…OK…OK…keep us posted. Thanks, Lou." She turned to the others. "Alex is at home with his—what's the PC way to say it?"

Billy helped her out. "Parents. Mothers. Caregivers. Whatever."

"And Randy?" Amy asked.

"Alex says he's fishing with his dad. Lou's checking that out. There's no one home, though he left several messages on their home voicemail and on their cell phones. On the river, though, they may not have cell phone reception. He's trying to find them in eastern Washington tonight. They float the Yakima so they'll likely be staying in or around Ellensburg.

If they're not at any of the local motels, he'll put out an APB and check with Randy's father's office first thing tomorrow morning."

"This doesn't pass the smell test," Abe softly said.

"Lou's calling back soon. Let's only cross that bridge if we have to. Don't you think?" Corey asked.

"Yes, absolutely, but if we haven't heard from Lou in fifteen minutes, one of us should call him again. In the meantime, what did I miss?"

"Billy and Amy have been telling me about Sara and Peter," Corey replied. "Peter, apparently, was so charismatic that he was accepted by the *"popular crowd "*—she raised the first two fingers of each hand on either side of her head, mimicking quotation marks—even though he wasn't one of them, or even interested in them."

"They actually courted him." The corners of Amy's mouth turned up, just barely, as she remembered. "They'd drive him around when he didn't have a car, buy his coffee at the Blue City, whatever he wanted."

"I get that he's charismatic, but there has to be more to this," Abe mused. "From what Billy's said, the popular crowd doesn't often reach out or bend their rules."

"I didn't really know Peter," Billy said. "Amy, can you explain this?"

"I'll try." She pursed her lips, steepled her fingers, concentrating. "Okay, Peter has it all, the whole package—smart, sensitive, sexy and charming. But the most important, the quintessential"—she winked at Billy, who liked that word—"the quintessential thing is that he's absolutely, totally, fearless..." Amy let this drift, remembering, before going on, "...and one way or another, the guy manages to think his way out of anything."

"Can you give us an example?" Corey asked, encouraging her.

"Sure. There are lots of stories. Here's one I actually saw myself. It was during my sophomore year. Peter was a junior, and we were hanging near a low wall in a parking lot off Broadway. I watched how he stood up to four older guys—tough, Asian gang guys—who wanted money from Jake, one of our classmates. One of these bullies, the leader, had a bat, another one had a piece of lead pipe. Peter asked them to back off. When they didn't, he took a step closer and told them to back off. I thought these guys were going to kill him. One of them kicked Jake's legs out from under him, causing him to take a hard fall on the concrete. When they laughed and came closer, Peter took a thin metal pen from his jacket pocket and said, 'OK, I'm going to write you a check, pay you off. You can cash it right there.' He nodded toward a bank on the corner. They looked over at the bank, and before anyone realized what he was doing, he had this steel pen up the gang leader's nose, poised to pierce his brain and kill him."

"'Drop the bat,' Peter ordered, and everyone watched it fall to the pavement. Back off now, all of you, or this pen goes into this bonehead's brain." Peter had this crazy look on his face that made it unmistakably clear that he was ready to kill him, period. The tough guy was standing on his tip toes, gasping, waving everyone away. Peter told Jake to call 911. He didn't take the pen out of the gang guy's nose until the cops arrived... That was Peter. I could tell you story after story—like how he and Randy unleashed the plagues at Olympic: grasshoppers, snakes, cockroaches, rats, and so on. He was fearless, he never got caught, and he could figure his way out of—well—whatever. Peter was just Peter, and everyone wanted to be his friend."

"Okay. I get this now." Abe said. "Did Peter know Snapper?"

"Absolutely," Amy replied. "They were together—partners, lovers—before Peter left."

"Oh my god," Corey jumped in. "That explains the book I found with Snapper's things." She told them how and where she found it. "I'll get it and show it to you." She left the room.

"This is helpful, and, I think, important," Abe reflected. "How did Peter meet Snapper?"

"I think Randy introduced them," Amy replied. "Randy knew Snapper first, though I can't say how."

Corey came in with the book, *The Bull From the Sea* by Mary Renault. She turned the book over and read from the blurb on the back that it told the story of Theseus, King of Athens. She read, "It opens with his triumphant return from Crete after slaying the Minotaur." She stopped reading. "So what happens when he comes home? And, could it be relevant to our frightening, maddeningly inexplicable problems?"

"I'm guessing it's part of the complex web of events that Sara is investing with present day meaning," Abe offered. "Though I don't really understand what she's trying to tell me."

"Can you tell us the rest of the story, just what happened?" Billy asked.

"I don't know if, or how, it's relevant, but his return ends tragically," Abe explained. "Before he left for Crete, his mortal father, Aegeus told Theseus to put up white sails if he was successful in killing the Minotaur. The trip back was difficult, and Theseus, distressed, forgot to put up the white sails. When his father saw the black sails, he jumped from a cliff into the sea and drowned, thinking his son had been slain."

"Dark...sad," Billy observed.

"Like something Sara would tell," Amy added.

Corey opened the book and showed them the inscription, "For Snapper. Love, Peter."

Amy asked if she could see the book and Corey gave it to her. Amy leafed through it, curious.

The phone rang. Abe hurried to answer it. "Lou...yes...yes...I see... that's good news. Thanks."

"Lou got a call back from Randy's dad. They're just coming from the river to the Ellensburg Inn. Lou confirmed with the Inn that they were holding a room for them for late arrival."

"I'm relieved," Corey said.

Abe frowned, his eyebrows coming together in a V that Corey and Billy recognized; he was concentrating, really focused. "I hesitate to say this, but I think whoever killed Snapper—and I'm convinced he was murdered—is very smart. And I believe Sara when she says the Beast isn't finished yet. Until now, I didn't know that Peter and Snapper and Randy were so closely connected. I need to talk with Sara about this first thing tomorrow morning. I'm going to call Lou back, make sure he understands all of this."

"Forget your smell test. This smells like spoiled fish, skanky," Billy proclaimed. "Ask Lou to actually see Randy, or, at the very least, talk with him, in the morning."

Amy leaned closer to Billy and whispered in his ear, "I'm starting to get why I love you."

◆◆◆

Sara was tossing and turning in the bed in her hospital room. She looked out of her window. It was still dark outside. There was a noise in the hallway, a subtle tapping on her door. She sat up in bed, checked the clock—5:00 a.m. The door creaked open, slowly. First, she saw his shadow, then there he was...*the Beast*. He wore a long, black, leather greatcoat. A black scarf covered the lower half of his face. Under the scarf, he wore a nylon mask that made his features unrecognizable.

He raised his hands above his head hitting his marks just so. When he finished his Cretan Bull dance his fingers hung in the air, like horns, beside his temples.

Sara screamed, but no sound came out, and then he was gone. She rang repeatedly for the nurse. When two nurses finally came, they insisted that she must have been dreaming. No one else had seen the creature in black.

CHAPTER NINE

Abe arrived at the hospital at 5:30 a.m. It was twenty minutes after Sara called, distraught, to tell him that she'd seen the Beast, that he'd visited her room, that he'd danced some kind of Cretan Bull dance. Even though she was practically hysterical, and gasping, Sara was so specific that he believed her.

When Abe opened her door, Sara was crying. She was sitting up in bed with her arms wrapped around her shoulders, sobbing inconsolably.

Abe sat on the bed beside her. "Did you see the Beast?"

Sara nodded twice—yes, yes—emphatically.

"Did you recognize him?'

She shook her head, no. "Where's Peirithous?"

"Randy?"

"Peirithous," she insisted. "Theseus' best friend, Peirithous."

Her encounter with the Beast—real or imagined—had frightened her, and she was disoriented, unfocused. She had, he could already see, lost some of the ground that they'd recently gained together. He tried to bring her back. "If it's Randy you're asking about, he's in Ellensburg with his dad, fishing on the Yakima River."

"Where's Peirithous?" She repeated. "Where? He's in danger unless I find Theseus. Right away!"

Sara was regressing into her mythological world, letting go of the fragile connection they'd recently forged. If it was the Beast's intention to make it harder for Abe to reach her, then he was succeeding.

Abe put his arm around her, consoling her. "We will find Theseus. We'll find him, and we'll save Peirithous. Let's talk in the morning. I'm going to get you some medication that will help you sleep and I'm going to sit with you until you're sleeping soundly."

Abe rang for the nurse, organizing a sleeping pill for Sara. When she was tucked in, he sat in a chair beside the bed and explained that he was going to get police protection for her.

He had a bad feeling and called Lou, "Sorry to wake you...did you call the Ellensburg Inn again? Check to see if he showed up...I'm guessing he didn't...let's put police protection on all of the kids...twenty-four seven...right away...let's keep them home from school...if you can't find them in Oregon, call Randy's father's office when it opens..." Abe smiled. "I know you already thought of that...call me back when you know anything..."

♦♦♦

Minos was staring down at Randy. It was 7:30 a.m. and the sun was shining into his lab. The top knuckles on Randy's forth finger and pinky finger were broken, crushed. They were bruised, black and blue, and swollen. The Cretan Bull's knuckles used to look like that after a long, hard fight.

Randy's mouth was covered with duct tape, and Unlucky Red was moaning through the tape. Tears flowed onto his cheeks. Minos sedated him, and watched the redheaded boy slip into unconsciousness.

He felt better. He'd talked with Not-so-Lucky Red. During the conversation, Minos used his pliers to crush the boy's knuckle. That's all it took. Not-so-Lucky Red told him everything. After the first knuckle, he believed everything he said. The way the boy told it, Snapper gave him a book, told him it was protection, "proof" he called it. He said "just show it to Sara if I ever have a problem." He had never shown it to Sara, because Red couldn't find it. The redheaded hotty swore to God that he'd never even opened the book. What god, Minos wondered. Red would have been more convincing if he'd named Zeus.

At first Unlucky Red insisted that someone had stolen the book from his backpack, along with some pictures that were missing. Minos knew about the pictures, but he didn't steal the book. So he got his pliers and broke that pinky-finger knuckle. When Red finally stopped screaming and crying, Minos walked him through the rest of that day. It was when he set the pliers and threatened to break the second knuckle, that Unlucky Red remembered giving a book to the girl in the café. Maybe he gave her the wrong book, he theorized. There it was. Of course. It was that same lanky girl, who was with the boy he didn't like, the nosey one who looked right at him when he was smoking on the street.

He had made his sacrifice to Zeus in her squirrelly boyfriend's room. Just thinking about that nasty couple made him mad. And he was mad that he hadn't thought to check out the long-legged girl's books before. Stupid, silly Minos, he scolded himself. No wonder the Master was angry. Okay, he'd fix this soon enough, fix it once and for all. He'd take care of nosey Billy and his long-legged girlfriend. He had time to do it, yeah. She had the "proof," yes, but she had no idea that she had it, what it actually meant, or whom to show it to. The only one who knew what to do was Randy. And Unlucky Red was out of the picture.

Minos taped their photographs, side by side, on his mirror... squirrelly Billy and his lanky twist...

He frowned, confounded. Minos wasn't sure how he'd play his game with both a boy and a girl.

It came to him then—like all of his best ideas—it was just there: his father, the Cretan Bull, and his sister, the sullied Devil Whore.

He was five years old when his father killed his wild and beautiful seventeen-year-old half-sister, Ariadne. Her mother, a gypsy, had left her with the Cretan Bull, after their youthful romance. He named her for King Minos' lovestruck daughter who helped Theseus kill the Minotaur and escape from the Labyrinth. He remembered the day his father discovered that Ariadne was having an affair with his diseased wife's brother, the married, fifty-year-old harbor master. He'd slapped her, savagely. Ariadne fell back and cracked her head against the edge of a stone table. She had died instantly.

His father wrapped her in a blanket and put her in the back of their beat-up Ford panel van. They drove to their fishing boat, bound her with a heavy chain, and dumped her out at sea. From that day on it was just the two of them. His father never spoke his daughter's name again. She was simply the sullied—the unclean—Devil Whore.

Minos made a sad face and sang, "Eenee, meenee, minee, mo… killed my sister…no…no…no…"

◆◆◆

Young Minos was back on the boat with his father, his babaka. As they cast their nets, The Cretan Bull liked to tell his young son about Minoan Crete— the gods, the heroes, and the kings—especially Minos, his namesake.

When King Minos died, the gods rewarded him in the afterlife. He became a judge of the souls of the dead in Hades. The three judges decided whether a soul went to Tartarus, a great abyss, a dank, gloomy pit, a prison of eternal torment and suffering; The Asphodel Meadows, a vast plain of Asphodal flowers, where ordinary souls were sent; or Elysium, a paradisal realm, a place for the distinguished, like Achilles or Socrates. Minos was the judge of the final vote. Okay, he'd send nosey Billy and his unclean Devil Whore to Tartarus. He smiled at that idea, thinking how Minos' father, Zeus, sent his own father, Cronus, there along with the rest of the Titans. One of the Titans, Atlas, was sentenced to hold the sky on his shoulders. Another, Prometheus, was chained to a mountain with an eagle feeding on his regenerating liver. Young Minos cringed.

The Furies often supervised the torture and punishments in Tartarus. They specialized in avenging crimes against the natural order, especially people who murdered family members.

He imagined his own father, the Cretan Bull, being tortured relentlessly by these wretched, foul-smelling hags. The Furies had bat's wings, snakes for hair and blood dripping from their eyes. In his mind's eye he could see them brutally beating his father with their brass-studded scourges. Yes, it would be unbearably humiliating for the Cretan Bull to be at the mercy of these hideous women, forever.

"Eenee, meenee, minee, mo…babaka, babaka…" His face hardened. *"You reap what you sow."*

◆◆◆

Minos' mind settled in a good groove, and then he was back in the present. He watched the boy now, sleeping soundly.

Minos sat beside him, at his lab table, turned on the Skytron Halogens, adjusted them so the light was just right, then picked up the foam latex makeup appliance from where he'd set it on the table. Minos began fitting it to the boy's face. When he had it just so, Minos compared the mask to the last picture of his father, the Cretan Bull, lying face up, on his back on the canvas, just after his last fight—the fight that had killed him. His babaka was killed two days after his birthday. Minos had just turned nine.

Randy's death mask was already a good likeness, but the reopened scar, and the cuts and the bruising around both brows needed more detailing. Finally, he needed to mix fresh blood. The battered, blood-streaked face had to be just right. With his syringe, then the extra-fine paintbrush, Minos applied another layer of liquid latex to the top portion of the boy's scar. While it was drying, he turned to his RMG appliance color wheels. He chose the injury/FX wheel to begin his work on the brows. He'd start with warm honey, then add maroon and thunder grey. The blood would be the last, finishing touch—painted on sparingly—a grace note. His secret was adding chocolate syrup to the other ingredients in his blood mix at the end. The syrup was a wet thickener and it added a realistic deep maroon, venous color to the blood. He felt better. This was, he decided, his favorite game.

In his mind, Minos was already seeing the mask he'd fashion for his beautiful sister, the Devil Whore. He looked over at the mask he was finishing, Randy's death-mask, a perfect likeness of the Cretan Bull's ravaged face...*Beauty and the Beast.*

◆◆◆

"Yes, Lou." Abe was sitting in the corridor, outside of Sara's room. There was a policeman standing near her door. "Randy's dad, Frank, cancelled the room at the Ellensburg Inn? He said they were driving on to the Deschutes, in Oregon? No, this isn't tracking... Frank's office has him on business in New York City? So you've put police protection on Sara, Billy, Amy and Alex...and an APB on Randy... I'll call Owen, their counselor, and see if anyone else needs to be warned... I'm at the hospital... I'll call

Jim Peterson, Sara's father, right away… Please bring Sara's things to my office…she'll need them when I see her at nine thirty…yes, Lou, even the cauldron…"

"Jim, Abe Stein." Abe was pacing now, in the corridor outside of Sara's room. "Randy's missing… I've put police protection on all of the kids, including Sara… She says the Beast came into her room last night… I don't think she was dreaming or fantasizing…no, I don't have any proof…let's have this conversation in person…Sara's sleeping…I gave her a sleeping pill…she should be up soon… I'll see you here…"

◆◆◆

Ten minutes later, Abe poked his head in to see Sara, sitting up in bed, looking out the window. "Peirithous is in danger," she announced.

"Yes, I believe he is," Abe agreed. "Here's what I'd like to do. Your father's coming. He'll check you out of the hospital and take you home. I want you to meet me at the office in an hour." He checked his watch. "At nine-thirty. I asked Lieutenant Ballard to bring all of your things to the office before then."

"What things?"

"Whatever you'll need to reach the Oracle. We're going to raise Theseus. You and I, together. We have to."

"My father will try to stop me."

"We can't let that happen. You're right. Lives are at stake. I'll talk with him. Try to argue for one last session. I'll organize it so that he can come when we're done. I know he'll want that."

"And if he won't agree?"

"Can you sneak out?"

"No prob."

"I'll pick you up on that bench near Olympic."

"What about the police?"

"I'll work that out. In fact, if necessary, I'll have Lieutenant Ballard pick you up and bring you to the office himself."

"You are rockin' doc. What happened?"

"I'm afraid you have to know this. Randy—Peirithous—is missing."

"Oh god…oh my god…" Sara started crying, then she curled up in a fetal ball on the bed.

"We have to find Theseus." Abe put a hand on her shoulder. "Sara, we can do this—you and I—together."

Jim opened the door. "Abe?"

Abe led him into the hall, closed the door. Sara was still crying on the bed.

In the hospital corridor, Jim turned to face Abe. He wore a doctor's white coat over his suit and tie. Jim looked weary, worn down and sad. "I've been thinking about you," he began, firm.

Abe braced for bad news.

Jim breathed from his inhaler. "Abe, this just isn't working. Sara's gotten progressively worse under your care, and I'm terribly worried about her, no, frightened for her."

"I do understand your frustration, your worries, even your anger—"

"No, I don't think you do. Abe, I'm sure you mean well, but what you're doing is demonstrably bad for Sara. She's coming undone. Last night she cut herself three times. She almost bled to death. The nurse confirmed that Sara swore she saw a monster in her hospital room just before dawn. That's an hallucination—"

"Jim, she's my patient and I need more time. You have no way of judging how the treatment is working—"

"Maybe, but she's my daughter and she's losing her connection to the world."

"Here's all I ask: one more session. After, the three of us will talk about everything. I'd like to see her at nine-thirty this morning. You can join us once we've finished. We'll answer your questions, review and evaluate our work together. After we talk, you can think through next steps."

"I'll think about this. I sincerely hope you can convince me that you're helping my daughter. I'll call you."

"A question you could help me with in the meantime. Did Peter say what time he was calling?"

"He's supposed to call tomorrow at eleven a.m."

"Can I talk with him?"

"Of course."

"Thank you. Let me say good bye to Sara." Abe left Jim in the hall.

He sat on the bed next to Sara, who was still crying and, he guessed, withdrawing even further. "Sara, listen carefully. If your father doesn't agree to let us meet at the office—and I don't think he will—meet me at the bench at nine fifteen. Okay?"

Sara squeezed his hand. "I'll be there," she whispered, between her sniffles and moans.

♦♦♦

Amy called Billy at 8:00 a.m. She asked him to come over, right away. She had something to show him. Corey knew the police officer that Lou had assigned to Billy, and she convinced him to drive Billy to Amy's. Yes, it would make her feel better, more comfortable anyway, she explained to Ralph, the policeman. When they arrived at Amy's, Ralph waved at the police officer in the car in Amy's driveway.

Ralph walked Billy to Amy's front door at 8:05.

Amy opened the door and led him into their living room. "Something about the book your mom showed us last night made me remember this." She showed him a book she'd left on the coffee table, Mary Renault's *The King Must Die,* the sister volume to *The Bull from the Sea,* the book Corey had found in Snapper's squat. Amy opened it—this one was also inscribed to Snapper from Peter. "You remember when Randy loaned me a book for our art history project?"

Billy nodded.

"He gave me this book instead. I'm sure it was a mistake," she explained. Amy opened the book. At the back there was an envelope. She opened the envelope. In the envelope there was a drawing. It was a gravestone. On the stone someone had written, "MOIRA. EVEN THE KING MUST DIE." There was also a pendant in the envelope, a chain with a silver stallion. Amy took out the necklace.

"It's the same as the chain they found on Snapper."

Billy took out his phone, "Mom, find Dad. Amy found something important... It's another book that Peter inscribed to Snapper. Only there's an envelope with this one… In the envelope there's a drawing and a stallion pendant… We'll bring it to the house in five minutes."

◆◆◆

Jim was driving Sara home. A police car followed them. Sara was still crying in the front seat. "I want to see Dr. Stein," she said. "Right away… I have to."

"I'm not sure that's a good idea. Things keep getting worse, not better."

"Sometimes things have to get worse before they can get better. Peirithous is in danger. He needs my help."

"I understand. How about this? Peter's calling tomorrow. Why don't you talk everything over with him. I'm sure he can help you think this through. After, if you still want to see Dr. Stein, we'll arrange it."

"Please let me see him today. One last time. Then I'll talk it over with Peter."

"I'm sorry, Sara. I'm not saying you can't see him again, but please rest today. Let's revisit this tomorrow after you talk with your brother."

"Okay…fine," Sara said, thinking *Okay, she'd have to sneak out. There was no other way.*

◆◆◆

Abe, Lou Ballard, Billy, and Amy all arrived at the house at the same time. Sam, Abe's driver, was so flustered that he drove onto the grass on their front lawn to avoid hitting Lou's police car as it pulled into the driveway.

Abe ushered them all inside, where Corey was waiting.

"Show them the book and the envelope," Billy said to Amy.

She gave the envelope to Corey. "Randy gave this to me, by mistake." Corey took out the drawing and the stallion necklace. She showed it to Abe.

Abe's phone rang. "Yes, Jim…another doctor? A second opinion? Please reconsider… I'm sorry you feel that way…your mind is made up…I see…" Abe shut off the phone.

"What now?" Corey asked.

"I need to see her. Lou, I'm going to need your help with that. You'll have to pull off her police protection, so she can sneak out. I'm supposed to pick her up at nine fifteen."

"I don't think that's legal." Lou frowned. "Un-unh."

Corey went on. "Will Sara know what the drawing and the necklace mean?" she asked.

"If anyone can tell us what they mean it's Sara. She wears this same necklace. OK. Lou, call off your guy, tell him to get coffee, doughnuts... whatever."

"Doughnuts, uh-huh." Lou smiled meanly. "Truthfully, I'm not surprised that her dad cut you off. I mean he's a *real* doctor."

Abe ignored him. "Please come by my office before nine o'clock with all of Sara's things...I'm going to need you to park in front of my office and keep her dad out, if he shows up before I'm ready."

"Ilegal." Lou cracked a knuckle. "For sure."

Abe shot Lou a zip-it look. "We're out of time."

Lou shrugged.

"Has anyone seen Randy?" Corey asked Lou.

"We've got an APB out for him. His picture's been posted and they're running it on the news. So far, no one's seen anything."

"So we don't have a clue. Nothing," Corey summed it up.

"You two—you're like world-class creep magnets." Lou cracked another knuckle. "We got that going for us."

"You friggin' gasbag..." Corey shook her head.

Billy and Amy exchanged a smile.

"So what are you thinking?" Corey eventually asked Lou.

"I'm guessing he, she, whatever's already on to the next target. Whoever's doing this knows we're clueless, and he's having too much fun."

Amy took Billy's hand, plainly anxious.

◆◆◆

Lou stepped into the kitchen to pick up his messages. Amy and Billy went upstairs. Abe was in his office. Corey came to the door and watched him. Abe had his feet on his desk, and he was pouring over his notes, written on little stick-ons pasted into Robert Graves' *The Greek Myths* and Edith Hamilton's *Mythology.*

Corey came over and put her hand on Abe's neck. "Sara's lucky," she said. "She has an exceptional doctor. A doctor who's willing to accept and work with her experience, what she sees and feels, even if it doesn't fit some diagnosis or even make sense."

Abe touched her hand. "Serious question. Something I'm worried about. This is moving very fast since we talked. I've accepted her reality, followed her into the past, but I'm still not connecting. How far should I go, babe?"

"What do you mean?"

"End of the day, I think this is an all or nothing deal. Sara's as smart as anyone I've ever met, and she doesn't miss a trick. But as I follow her into the past, I'm learning that she lives in this very bizarre and complicated world—a strange, dark, landscape of heroes, brave deeds, fierce monsters, and extremely harsh consequences. In her world a misstep can quickly lead to a curse, a self-inflicted wound, a terrible punishment, even death. The dilemma I'm wrestling with comes from your very good advice. You were right—to help Sara discover what I believe she knows, I have to enter her reality, actually experience it and engage it, participate in it, even when it gets crazy—and you know me, I don't use that word lightly. I have to help her reach the Delphic Oracle and raise Theseus. There will be obstacles along the way—unexpected demands and challenges, dark rites that I don't understand, with unpredictable outcomes. I'm just not sure how far to go. This is outside of what I know, what I'm comfortable with. I don't know how to explain it."

"Is this still therapy?"

"Yes and no. Structurally, it's very different—I need to trust her *completely*, follow her lead. Wherever it takes me. And she's all over the map. She says the Beast could be the Minotaur or a murderous white sow or the ferocious three-headed creature that guards the gates of Hell. She says it could be any and all of these monsters, and many, many more. She can detail the atrocities of each and every hideous creature, but in spite of my efforts, she can't make any link whatsoever to the present. None at all. She can predict the old coin under Snapper's tongue or explain the sacrifice to Zeus in Billy's room, but it's all about things that happened thousands of years ago. The deeper you go into her maze, into Sara's complex labyrinth, the more detail you learn about the past but you never get any closer to the present."

"So you've taken her lead, but she's not taking you where you need to go?"

"Something like that. Yes. We've been trying to raise the Delphic Oracle with fires and potions in my office. It's not enough. Still, the way I think about it is that I have to trust that she wouldn't keep trying to reach Theseus—and put herself in harms way—if she didn't desperately want to tell someone her elusive, terrible secret."

"You like her, don't you?"

"Very much."

"So keep it simple, don't overanalyze this...Sara sounds very crazy to me—at least that's what I would have said before I met you. Now, let's just say she's frightened—confused and disconnected—but I'm not sure that's what matters..." Corey lay her hand on his chest. "What's your gut?"

Abe didn't hesitate. "Sara's the real deal. She knows something terrifying, a hideous, inaccessible secret. She's fearlessly fighting deadly demons to protect her friends. I'm thinking that I have to stand alongside her."

Corey leaned in, whispered in his ear, "All the way, babe. You go all the way."

◆◆◆

"What if we're next?" Amy asked Billy. They were sitting side-by-side on his bed.

"We have police protection. We'll be careful, and, I promise you, my mom and dad will make sure we're safe. They'll be all over this."

"They've had some experience with this kind of stuff, haven't they?"

"Yeah. We were on the run, up the Inside Passage. Someone blew up our boat, tried to kill us. My mom and dad had to deal with the guy behind it."

"Deal with?"

"My dad shot him, killed him."

"Your dad, the brainy shrink, did that?"

"Yeah. Took everyone by surprise—even my mom thought they were both going to die." Billy nodded. "And you remember when Maisie and Aaron were kidnapped. My mom and dad kidnapped Teaser's daughter, traded her for Aaron and Maisie. My mom was way ahead of that, and no one at Olympic would even listen to her."

"Olympic…agh! Today, I made a promise to myself that when this is finally over, I'm going to stop Dave and his crew from hassling Sara. She's had enough trouble. Bullying Sara is just not okay."

"Did talking about Peter make you think about that?"

"It got me thinking about standing up to bullies. Though truthfully, I'm not sure how to stop Dave and his friends. I don't think there's anything we can say that will back them off."

"I'll help. We'll figure it out, do it together." He took her hand.

"Yes, yes we will." She kissed him, a long tender kiss.

Amy put her arm around his neck. "I like your parents, though they seem like an unlikely couple."

"That's what people say about us."

CHAPTER TEN

Sara was in the basement, lying on their big, soft couch, watching TV. She had a comforter spread over her and two pillows under her head. Her dad poked his head in. He had a tray with breakfast—eggs, bacon, toast, butter and jam. Jim set the tray on the couch beside Sara. "Everything okay?" he asked.

Sara muted the TV. "Thanks, Dad." She smiled at him. "I'm better than okay...you were right. I needed to veg out, turn off my mind. If I can, I'll nap after breakfast."

"Whatever you'd like. I'm going to the hospital to see patients. I'll be back by noon to have lunch with you. In the meantime, I've invited the police officer to sit upstairs in the kitchen and have coffee. He'll keep an eye on you. I asked him to check in with you. If you need anything, he'll help you."

"That's good. Thanks. See you at noon."

Sara turned the TV back on, ate some eggs, bacon and toast. When she heard her father's car leave the driveway, she was up, fully clothed, even in her sneakers, and out the basement door in a flash. It was 9:05.

◆◆◆

At 9:15, the burgundy Olds with the neat white trim, pulled up, slowly and carefully, to the bench in front of the Olympic Academy. Abe was driving. Sara was sitting on the bench, waiting. As soon as she saw the car, Sara was up and in the front seat.

"I thought you didn't drive."

"I don't. This is an exception. Everything about today has been an exception. Sam, my driver, was out and we don't have time to waste. Are you okay?"

"If you can get us to the office, I'm good to go."

"I drove to my office earlier, to set up your things. On the way, I clipped a side mirror off a parked car," Abe pulled away from the curb, lurching.

Sara winced.

"Don't say anything. I need to concentrate."

◆◆◆

Across from the office, Abe parked in a parking lot. They ran past Lou, who was double parked in front of the Chinese restaurant under the viaduct. Abe and Sara hurried up the stairs. In the office, Sara's magic circle was uncovered. Her tripod and cauldron stood in the center of her circle. Abe had already set the candles in place. Her canvas shoulder bag and her duffle sat beside the circle.

Sara went to work, unpacking and organizing the things she'd need. Abe opened the window on the alley side so she could light her propane fire and her candles. Sara prepared her potion, the same potion she'd used in the woods. As she sprinkled in herbs, she chanted, "I call on Poseidon, the fierce and the beautiful…I must find Theseus, I cannot be denied…"

Her potion was starting to bubble in her cauldron. Abe watched Sara light her candles at each of the five points of the star where they touched the edge of her circle. Next, she added more wine, more herbs and rock salt to her potion. When she was satisfied, Sara drank from her vial of wine, honey, chopped cheese, and meal. Abe stepped into the circle beside her. When she offered him her Ambrosia, he drank it down, too.

With her Athame, Sara cut off a piece of meat from the lamb shank. She handed it to Abe. He lowered it into her cauldron. "I sacrifice this baby lamb to you great Apollo, god of truth and prophecy."

Sara raised her Athame above her head. Softly she whispered, "I am the priestess, the vestal virgin. I pray to the Oracle, servant of Apollo. I must find Theseus. I need him now…" She drank more ambrosia, the divine nectar of the gods.

Abe drank more ambrosia, too, then he began chanting, "I call on Paian Apollo, on Zeus the cloud gatherer, and on great Poseidon, who speaks like the sea...help us find Theseus, we need him now..."

◆◆◆

Minos attached the foam latex appliance to Randy's face. He adjusted the thin black mustache until it was just so, then Minos hid the edges of the appliance with a light coat of liquid latex. He compared it to his picture of the Cretan Bull. The death mask was almost finished, though he still needed to mix, then add, the fine, deep-red streaks of blood.

Minos pulled back Randy's long red hair. With a sharp scissors, he began cutting it off. The wavy red hair fell to the floor. Minos liked the feel of Red's hair, the texture, and he continuously ran his hand through the wavy red hair as he cut it off. When he was satisfied that it was short enough, Minos stood, facing the mirror.

Next to Billy's picture, he'd taped a photo of the Cretan Bull—he'd chosen an image of his father lying dead in his coffin. Next to Amy's picture he'd taped a photo of Ariadne, the Devil Whore. It was taken on her sixteenth birthday. She was very happy that day and very beautiful. He smiled, already anticipating his next game. He'd send Unlucky Red's soul to the Underworld today, and begin this new game tomorrow.

He took out an ancient silver coin, an obolus that he would place under Red's tongue when he was finished. He set the old Greek coin on the table. He wondered how Minos the King would cast his vote for Randy's dead soul.

Minos looked down at the carefully-crafted death mask. He'd fashioned a perfect likeness. Red *was* the horribly battered Cretan Bull as he lay, dead, on the canvas.

The Master would be pleased and proud.

◆◆◆

Sara drank her Ambrosia, letting it run down her chin as Abe called, "Blue-haired Poseidon, master of ships and stallions, you who sired him, lead us to Theseus. I call on Theseus. The Beast is rising. We need him now…" As he called, Sara swayed, her Athame held high.

She stepped closer to the cauldron. Sara was chewing a laurel leaf now, to help induce a trance. She swayed back and forth, eyes on the boiling potion. "Accept my offering, great Apollo, keeper of light," Sara chanted. "And to you, Poseidon, breaker of ships and cities, I offer again to you, to appease your anger."

Abe added another piece of lamb to the bubbling cauldron.

Sara cried out, "Take me. I am your vessel. Let me cry out your prophecy." Sara swayed and twirled, "Let me cry out your prophecy," she repeated.

Then louder, "I wait…your humble servant…but you give me nothing…nothing…" Sara raised both arms about her head. "Nothing! You grant me nothing!" She lowered her hands, raised them again. "Very well…" And louder still, "Then there must be blood. The gods must dance in blood!"

Abe stepped forward, chanting, "I call on Theseus. We need you now…"

"There must be blood," Sara cried. "The gods must dance in blood." She raised her Athame. As she began to bring it down, Abe grabbed her wrist.

"There will be blood," he said, taking the Athame, and before Sara understood what he meant, Abe forced his sport coat and shirt sleeve up on his left forearm and brought the Athame down and across his exposed skin. Abe let the blood run down his forearm into the cauldron. "I call on Theseus," he chanted, squeezing even more blood from the wound. "We need you now…"

Sara twirled, triumphant. She leaned down gracefully scooping a silver goblet from her duffle. She dipped it in the simmering cauldron, set it down to cool, then she continued her swaying, twirling, and chanting. Her face was radiant, her eyes bright, and there were beads of sweat on her brow. "I call on Poseidon, the fierce and the beautiful…"

Abe joined in, "I call on Apollo, the truth teller…" He waited, watching Sara. Nothing yet. Abe took the silver cup, sipped from the heavy potion. "We wait on Theseus…help us now…" he cried out. Abe handed the silver cup to Sara.

Sara drank the potion, took another laurel leaf, then she called out, "I am the Pthyia, your vestal virgin, take me great Apollo…"

Abe chose this moment. He brought a chair into the circle, steadied Sara, then sat her in the chair. He handed her the Mary Renault book that Amy had given him, *The King Must Die*. "Randy mistakenly gave this book to Amy." Abe showed her the inscription. "There was an envelope at the back of the book. This was in it." Abe handed her the sketch.

Sara studied the sketch carefully. "MOIRA. EVEN THE KING MUST DIE," she whispered.

Abe gave her the chain with the silver stallion.

She fingered the stallion, eyes closed, then looked at the sketch again. She shook her head slowly, side to side. Her eyes lost their focus as she stood, swaying, in some sort of trance. She began shaking, tremors coursing through her body. Sara tilted her head back, eyes widening, then she cried out, a plaintive, piercing wail, then again. And again. Over and over. When she had no voice left, Sara slumped to the floor, crying softly.

Abe stood behind her, hands on her shoulders. Tears flowing down her cheeks, she murmured, "The King is dead. Theseus is dead…"

Abe waited.

"The King is Dead… Theseus is dead…" Sara repeated.

"How do you know?" Abe softly asked.

After a long silence, Sara took his hand, turned her head up to look at him. Tears flowed down her cheeks. She stared at him, squeezing his hand, shaking her head back and forth slowly. Her crying intensified, then she lowered her head. Later, Sara looked up at him again, taking deliberate breaths. Finally, she whispered, "Peter is dead…" Then again, "Peter is dead…"

It was what Abe had suspected, but hearing it was chilling. "Peter, your brother, is dead?" he asked.

Sara nodded. "This is his stallion."

"Can you be sure?"

Sara bowed her head, took slow, deep breaths. "Yes, I'm sure." Sara covered her face with her hands, moaning.

"Take your time, Sara." Abe massaged her shoulders.

Sara raised her head, massaging her own temples with her forefingers. When she was finally able to speak, she slowly, softly said, "I need to tell you a story."

"Please." Abe nodded.

Sara took more long breaths, composing herself; when she was ready she began, "When Theseus was seven, Hercules came to dine in Troezen." Sara nodded. As she relaxed into the past, telling her story, she became more poised. "Hercules removed his lion skin and threw it over a stool. When the palace children came in they all fled from the lion. All, that is, except seven-year-old Theseus who returned with an ax to kill the lion."

Abe watched her, worried that he'd lose her again in the past.

She went on, carefully, "The first time Peter told that story to me and the Horseman, he, Snapper—"

Abe nodded, relieved; she was back, and she'd made a connection.

"The Horseman asked Peter why Theseus took so many dangerous risks. 'How could anyone be so completely fearless? How was that possible?' The Horseman wanted to know. Volunteering to fight the Minotaur, hunting the murderous sow... He explained that he was asking Peter this question because Peter was just like Theseus. Peter was the only other person he knew that was genuinely fearless. What was it about Theseus that made him that way? Where, Peter, does it come from?" She hesitated, remembering. "I was there when he asked that...Peter thought about it then replied simply, 'Here's what Theseus believed.' Peter paused, wanting to get this just right. 'It's all Moira. Even the King must die.'"

Abe sat beside her until she was steady again, then he helped her back into the chair, where he gave her a handkerchief to wipe her eyes.

"So Peter said these very words."

"Yes, I was there."

"What did Peter mean?"

Sara closed her eyes, still tearful. When she was ready, she explained purposefully, "I've thought about that. Here's what Peter meant—it's all fate. Finally, even the king will die, but his fate or his Moira will determine when… If you truly believe in Moira, and Peter certainly did, then fear recedes. You can take risks, knowing the outcome is out of your hands. The more often you succeed, the easier it gets. Fear slips away. Since we were kids, Peter liked to pretend he was Theseus. Figuring out what Theseus was thinking, how he'd react, in dangerous, difficult situations was part of that. By the time Peter was thirteen, he could think like Theseus, be Theseus." She lowered her head again, massaged her temples.

"I think I understand."

She raised her head. "…I bet you have a boat load of psycho mumbo jumbo for that."

"Yes, I do."

Sara thought she saw a twinkle in his eye. She wiped away a tear, then sighed, rueful, "Anyway, after, we made a pledge, a pact, that 'Moira. Even the King Must Die,' would be Peter's epitaph."

"So can you tell me what the sketch means?"

Sara sighed, so sad, then forced herself to continue. "I think it's Peter's gravestone. It has to be. The Horseman wrote his epitaph on it. It was our secret, a promise we had together. And, of course, the stallion was Peter's. I had the black one, Snapper had the other silver stallion. Poseidon's stallions were the Horseman's gift to Peter and to me."

"So Peter is our modern-day Theseus. The person you were hoping to find to save your friends."

Sara took a careful breath. "Yes…I had no idea that he was dead…I couldn't even conceive of that possibility…oh my god…I was blind…" She began crying again. "I didn't get it…I wouldn't let myself…I didn't understand any of this until you showed me the book, the drawing and the stallion…and now…agh, I'm heartsick…" Without ever being aware of it, Sara had pressed her right hand to her left breast.

"I understand…and though you'll need time to grieve, Sara…for now, we need to concentrate on finding Randy…please…can you do that?"

She took several slow breaths. "I'll try…as horrible as this is—and Jesus, I feel like I could come undone at any moment—at the same time, it's like a weight has been lifted…"

"I get that. You've made a real connection, however sad, to the present. Hang on to that. Randy needs you."

Another breath. "Okay…though it's overwhelming me at the moment…it's hard to breathe…please help me…what do I do?"

"Sara, you've helped me understand half of the equation—Theseus, the Horseman and Perithious, that's Peter, Snapper, and Randy. I suspected that, but I couldn't be sure. But the other half, the Beast, is still a terrifying mystery that we absolutely have to solve. Here's how you can help. You're recovering memories. If we ask the right questions we may uncover more than you think. Can you suggest a place to start?"

Sara shook her head, no. She wrapped her arms around her shoulders.

"Randy's life is at stake. We need to help him." He just didn't know how to do that. He knew who did. "Sara, let's find Randy. He needs us now."

Sara took his hand, leading him toward the cauldron. She drank from the silver goblet. "I call on Theseus…"

◆◆◆

Minos was shaving Randy's head. He had his electric razor, the fancy one he'd bought online, at the site that sold to barbershops. When he'd shaved Red's hair down to a bristly red stubble, Minos took out his father's vintage straight razor, the navy imperial razor that the Cretan Bull had used until the day he died.

Minos covered Red's stubble with the extra creamy shaving cream he'd prepared, then he began removing the stubble with the carefully honed straight-edged razor. This was a fun game because his father's razor was so sharp that the stubble came off like melted butter. The shaved areas of Red's head were smooth now, like a bowling ball. Minos smiled when he realized that he couldn't rightly call him Red anymore.

When Randy's entire head was smooth as a baby's bottom, Minos carefully fit the designer wig over the top of his shaved head. He'd had it made specially—a perfect match for the Cretan Bull's black curly hair in the photo he'd chosen for Randy's death mask. After the wig was properly attached, Minos began to paint delicate streaks of his deep-red blood mixture on Randy's mask. With his thin brush, Minos drew fine streaks of blood from the Cretan Bull's ghastly reopened scar, his nose, his brow, the corner of his eye, and finally, a winding line from his misshapen right ear down his neck.

Minos stood, admiring his work. Before long, he was studying the pictures of Amy and Ariadne—in the photos they were almost the same age—taped to his mirror. He was thinking through his next project, a mask for his half sister, the Devil Whore. Her mask would have to be his best work ever. He wanted to capture her radiant beauty. It was the least he could do for his loving sister, who raised him after his mother died in childbirth.

He could still picture Ariadne, splitting her skull on the stone table. And that brought back the Master killing his own lover. He felt a tremor, a frisson—this was the first time he could bring up this memory. It was eerily similar. The Master and his lover were quarreling. In a rage, the Master slapped his lover, who fell backward. The back of his lover's head cracked open on the sharp edge of the marble fireplace mantel. Minos likened it to a machete splitting open a coconut, only instead of milk inside there was blood. His lover died instantly. The Master needed him after that. And Minos was born.

Born to serve the Master without the Master ever knowing. Young Minos on the inside, his babaka, the Cretan Bull, on the outside. In his mind, the Cretan Bull's cruelty, his ruthless tactical intelligence, coexisted with the playfulness, the sweetness of young Minos, before his sister died.

Facing the mirror, Minos put on his black suede fedora, cocking it stylishly. He fingered the brim with a thumb and two fingers. He lifted his hat off his head, just barely, as he tilted his head down—a tip of the hat to the Master. "Chapeau," he whispered.

◆◆◆

Sara drank from the silver goblet. When she handed the goblet to him, Abe sipped the potion, too. Sara was sitting on the chair Abe had set in her circle, concentrating on something. She was oddly calm, listening carefully to some voice in her head. "I can hear him," she said to Abe. "Though it's very faint."

"Who are you hearing?" Abe asked. He was standing beside her chair in the circle.

"I'm not sure…" She stood and began chanting, dancing and twirling. "I call on Peter, " she said. "My dear brother, I need you now."

"Is it Peter's voice you're hearing?"

"No it's my own, I think, though Theseus' spirit is helping. I can sense him helping," she said, putting her fingers to her temples, concentrating again. "It's my own voice, though, telling me about Peter."

Abe wasn't sure what she meant, but it didn't matter. He suspected she was simply remembering things that fit the new facts.

Sara sat back in the chair, "Ask me questions, I think I can answer at least some of them now."

Abe brought a second straight-backed chair and set it beside hers in the circle. He sat. "Why did Peter leave?" Abe softly asked.

Sara nodded, chanting now, mumbling something. "He didn't leave. Peter would never leave me, his sister, his only family. He died. That's his gravestone in the sketch."

"How did he die?"

She thought about that. "I don't know."

"Tell me about Peter and Snapper?"

"They were lovers, and the best of friends. He would never leave Snapper either."

"Did Snapper know how he died?"

"I'd guess so, though I can't say for sure."

"Is there anything that you remember?"

"The day after Peter left, the smell was in the car."

"What smell?"

"The Beast smell."

"What did the Beast smell like?"

"I'm not sure."

"Was it your car?"

"Yes, the smell was in our car in the morning."

"What smell, Sara? You're great with smells."

Sara concentrated. "Okay...yes...minty..." She frowned, working hard to bring back specifics. "Like eucalyptus, mixed with sweat...and mint...no, menthol...it was menthol."

Abe wasn't sure what to make of that. He shifted gears. "When did you first notice that smell?"

"Ever?"

"Yes, first time ever."

"Crazy...the first time...okay...yes...I do remember...the very first time was an indelible memory...yes...it was nine years ago...it was just after my mother died... We were in London. I'd been to the British Museum where I saw the Lapiths and the Centaurs...They frightened me so much—the killing and the raping. I was six years old then, and I can still see them vividly. That night I couldn't sleep. I kept picturing the centaurs, the ravaging, the death and brutality. I opened my door, just a little. It was an apartment hotel and we had a living room. I peered through the door and two men were in the room, dancing and kissing. One of them had a mark on his cheek, a big beard and a thin black mustache. His hair was black and curly. I think they were drunk. He looked sweet and funny. It was a party. Drinking and dancing. Like Pan. I didn't recognize either of them. I came out and said, 'Hello, who are you?' The man with the beard said he was my father. That it was time for bed. I thought he was joking, and I went back inside my room. When I asked my father about it in the morning, he said he didn't hear anything, that I must have been dreaming."

"Was Peter there? Did he hear anything?"

"No, he slept through it. When we talked about it later, though, we decided it was his other father Poseidon, looking after me. He was already pretending to be Theseus. And it was the beginning of our game. And remember Peter had two fathers, one of them a man of the sea, like Poseidon."

Abe let this sink in.

"In the morning the smell was there."

"The same smell that was in the car?"

"Yes, she said. Eucalyptus and Menthol."

Abe went to the computer on his desk, did some searching. "Cold creams often have Eucalyptus," he suggested. "And menthol, too…"

"Cold cream. Yes, that's it." Sara smiled wide.

Abe sensed that something had turned for her.

◆◆◆

Minos was working on Randy's hands. Earlier, when Unlucky Red started pleading with him to let him go, when he insisted that he'd told him everything, that he'd never say a word, Minos had taped his mouth shut, crushed a second knuckle then sedated him, to shut him up.

Now he was working on the other knuckles and the rest of his hand.

Minos had his hand palettes, his sponges, his paintbrushes and a bruise wheel with his favorite colors. He was almost finished. He'd used intense red, translucent yellow, maroon, blue vein and earth brown.

When he'd put on the final touch, when he was finally satisfied with his work, Minos wheeled the cot into the spare room. He readied the syringe, loaded the queen of all poisons, Cerberus' foam, and gave Unlucky Randy the injection. His father, the Cretan Bull, had used the poison to hunt whales. He'd spear the whale with a poison tipped lance, paralyzing it and causing it to drown. Watching the whale drown always made young Minos sad.

Minos inspected the dead Cretan Bull one last time—his face, his hair, and finally his hands.

Minos looked carefully at his own hands, so graceful when he danced, his long delicate fingers—so different from the bruised battered hands of the Cretan Bull. Young Minos painted and danced for the Master. The Cretan Bull killed for him.

◆◆◆

Sara had stepped out of the circle, and she was sitting in the cherry-colored chair across from Abe's desk. Abe was leaning his backside against the edge of the desk, asking her question after question. Time, they knew, was running out.

"We're not getting any closer to Peirithous…Randy…" Sara said. "I'm frightened for him."

"I have an idea, but you have to be ready for it."

"Go for it. I'm feeling way better…"

"Elephant in the room?"

"I'm there. If Peter's dead, who is my dad talking to?"

"Yes, are you ready to ask him?"

"He'll freak out that I'm here."

"I'll have Lou—Lieutenant Ballard—calm him down."

"Your policeman friend?"

"Yeah, he's good at this kind of thing." Abe dialed Lou. "Come on up, we need your help." Abe hung up the phone.

Abe called the hospital. "Please page Dr. Jim Peterson. Tell him Dr. Stein is calling, and it's urgent…Jim…Sara and I need to talk with you. Right away…I'll explain later…she's here at my office…if you don't cool off, I'll send Lieutenant Ballard to bring you over…he'll arrest you if he has to…we'll be waiting…" Abe hung up the phone.

Sara grimaced. "I hope he brought a spare inhaler," was all she said.

"Do you think he has any idea that Peter isn't in Greece?" Abe asked.

"No. None at all. He'd never knowingly lie about that."

"I agree."

"I just don't get it…no…I may not see things the same way as my dad, but he's always been there…present, calm…not weird or crazy…" Sara closed her eyes, massaging her temples. "I'm getting a headache… you got some psycho mumbo jumbo covers this?"

"None…none at all…I don't have a clue about this…"

Abe and Sara were still discussing her dad when Lou opened the door.

Always a keen observer, Lou took in the magic circle, the cauldron, the candles, Abe's bloodied, bandaged arm. "What the fuck? I should arrest you," he said to Abe.

"For what?"

"Voodoo…black magic…crazy shit…I dunno…" Lou shook his head, extended his arm. "I guarantee you that this isn't in any head shrinker's play book."

"It works," Sara offered, ignoring Lou's bluster.

Lou nodded in her direction. "Point taken, young lady." Lou pointed a gnarly finger at Abe. "You and Cory give me the willies. I just got the call. Bud Park—Snapper—he was poisoned. It was a variant of that funky old poison you wrote down for me. The ME did his homework—he says the only post mortem indications are those of asphyxia. Anyway, you were right."

"No, Sara was right." Abe clarified. "Again…Lou, we've got no time. We have reason to believe that Sara's half brother, Peter, is dead. I'll fill you in later. Now, we just called Sara's father at the hospital. He's on his way here and he's enraged. He'll be angry and difficult, and I'll need you to calm him down. You're the man for that job."

Lou ignored him. He had his iPhone out and he was taking pictures of Abe's office. "This is priceless. This is going to come back to haunt you."

Abe pressed on, "If we're right, and Peter is dead, then I believe that Jim is somehow part of this—though he likely doesn't know that, nor even know how he's part of it—"

"Oh shit—excuse my French, young lady, but Dr. Whacko's going off the reservation again."

Abe ignored Lou, continuing, "Jim's an honest man, a good, caring father. I don't think he's lying. I don't think he's hiding anything intentionally. We're going to ask him about his son. I want you to follow him when he leaves."

"The witchdoctor shrink has another loopy play up his sleeve." Lou chuckled. "I'm in."

"What did Corey call you Lou? A friggin' gasbag?"

Abe picked up the phone again. "Cor…we're making some progress…can you park near the office?…I may need you to drive me… pretty soon… We think Peter is dead…Sara's back, battered but intact… All the way, babe…"

◆◆◆

"Are you crazy?" Jim cried out, when Lou ushered him into Abe's office. Jim was pulling from his inhaler as he took in the witchcraft paraphernalia,

Abe's crudely bandaged and bloodied arm, and his daughter Sara, who was trembling, seated in her chair facing Abe's desk. Abe had moved his own chair and the extra chair in front of the desk so the three of them could talk. "How dare you?" Jim cried out. "I expressly forbade you to see my daughter, and—"

"Dad," Sara interrupted. "This is hard for all of us, but I'm doing better and we need your help. Forget what things look like and help me dad, please."

"Jim," Abe implored him. "Please sit down and hear us out. I think you'll want to know what Sara has figured out."

"Figured out? I hope this is very good, because it looks to me like you're encouraging my daughter's dark and destructive fantasies—driving her further and further from reality—"

"Dad, please sit down and let's talk."

Lou guided Jim toward the chair. "You're going to want to hear what they have to say, doctor. And they have questions that they need you to answer. Best to get it over with."

"You're going to answer for this, too, officer." Jim sat down grudgingly.

"Lou, will you please wait outside?" Abe asked.

"You sure?"

"Yeah, we're okay here. I'll call you if I need you."

Lou stepped out, closing the door behind him. Sara turned to her dad. She showed him the sketch, then the stallion. "The stallion belonged to Peter," she explained. "And the writing on the gravestone is the epitaph that Snapper and I promised that we'd write if he died. I think Snapper was killed because he knew that Peter was dead… Is that possible?"

"Peter dead? I don't know everything Peter is doing, but he's certainly been in touch with me. The postcards are real. It was his voice on the phone yesterday. As you know he's calling tomorrow. Both of you can talk with him then."

"Are you sure that it's Peter who's calling and sending the postcards?" Abe asked.

"I couldn't prove it, but it certainly sounds like his voice and it looks like his handwriting."

"Where exactly is Peter now?" Sara wanted to know.

"Somewhere in the Greek islands. Crete, I'd guess. But you know that already."

"Do you have any hard evidence that Peter's in Greece?" Sara persisted.

"You can ask him yourself tomorrow. Do you have any hard evidence that he isn't?"

"No," Sara admitted. "Just the drawing and the stallion...though as upsetting, as awful, as it is, I'm sure on this." Sara nodded, her face unbearably sad.

"Could you please wait until tomorrow—when he calls—before you make up your mind?"

Sara lowered her head, putting her face in her hands, trying to hold back her tears.

"Jim," Abe took a turn, giving Sara a chance to collect herself. "There's more. One of the things that Sara remembered was a night in London, when she was six years old. She couldn't sleep. She went into the living room of your hotel suite and saw two men dancing. One of them said he was her father, though he didn't look like you. In the morning, when she asked you about it, you told her that she'd been dreaming. Do you remember that?"

"Of course I do. Sara was still so upset about losing her mother, Niki. We all were. I made the mistake of taking her to the British Museum where she saw the Elgin Marbles. She had nightmares every night for weeks about the bloody battle between the Lapiths and the Centaurs at Peirithous' wedding. The raping and the killing traumatized her."

"Is it possible that she saw two men dancing in your hotel living room?"

"Unlikely, I was there and I didn't hear or see anyone. After talking with Sara in the morning, I checked again, and I didn't see any sign of anything unusual. It was more likely part of another nightmare. In the morning, she and Peter were talking about Peter's other father, Poseidon. I thought it was a game—make believe." Jim took another hit from his inhaler. "And now I have a question for you. Why in hell are you allowing my disturbed daughter to practice witchcraft in your office?"

Sara stood and faced him. "He's my doctor and he's helping me."

"This has gone too far. It's time to leave." Jim stood, facing Sara. "Sara?"

Abe stood, too. "Jim, please give us a chance. Sara's making progress. If you'll look at the facts, and look past the accoutrements of her process—" Abe made a gesture that included the circle and everything in it. "—what she's telling you about Peter, however tragic, is a hard-won connection to the present—"

"What exactly do you mean?"

"*Snapper* was murdered. *Poisoned*." Abe said forcefully. "Just as Sara insisted. We can prove that now. And yes, Randy's missing, just as Sara warned. How can you dismiss her warnings, her uncannily accurate predictions? And now, there's Peter."

"Sara wants Theseus to help her. How can you take that seriously?"

"Sara wanted Peter to help her, though she couldn't face the terrifying possibility that he was dead. In her mythological language, Theseus was Peter. But that's just the tip of the iceberg. I believe that if I continue to work with Sara, that she'll find the Beast, the murderer. I believe that Peter's death and the identity of his murderer is the terrible knowledge, the thing too hideous to bear, that made her disconnect, that drove her into the distant past, that forced her to create, then look for help in her own detailed mythological universe. If you let us keep working on it, we'll unlock her terrible secret."

"Dear God, you've become part of the problem. You believe this... you believe that...well, I believe that you're reckless and egotistical, and I believe that you've become dangerously, narcissistically invested in making Sara's mythological fantasies into something they're not. How can you reasonably encourage her baseless assertion that Peter, my son, is dead—without any proof! Sara can talk with Peter tomorrow. But Abe, we're going elsewhere for help. I'm afraid you're out of the picture." He turned to his daughter. "It's time to leave, Sara," he repeated, more forcefully.

Sara didn't move. "Dad, I'm sorry, but I'm staying right here. You don't have any idea what's best for me."

"I've had enough. Your care is finally my decision. Please come with me. Now."

"No! No! No! I'm actually getting better and you can't even see it. Go, now, before you ruin everything."

"I'll be back with my lawyer and a court order. And you"—Jim pointed a long finger at Abe—"You! Dear God, you're irresponsible and dangerous...I'm going to have your license revoked." Jim stormed out of the office.

◆◆◆

"Oh my god..." Sara said, then again, "Oh my god...my father can't even hear me...he can't even see that I'm better."

"He's in some kind of denial. I think he genuinely believes that Peter is alive in Greece, that he'll call tomorrow."

"And if he doesn't call?" Sara was crying now.

"He'll say he did, and he'll believe it...that's the piece I just don't understand..."

Sara's crying was intensifying.

Abe gave her a moment.

Sara sat down, collecting herself. "We're running out of time."

"Are you ready?"

"Not at all." She closed her eyes, massaged her temples with her forefingers. "But please go on," she insisted. "We have to." She was crying again.

"...Okay...Sara, do you think it's possible that your father knows the Beast...even if he isn't aware of it?..."

Something in her face changed, then Sara shook her head, no, raising a palm, trying to regain her composure. Through her tears Sara was barely able to say, a whisper, "No...no...my father doesn't know the Beast..." She put her face in her hands, gasping.

Abe waited, standing beside her, frowning with worry.

When she could, Sara looked over at him, despondent. "No... No... No!..." she managed. Then, standing, fists clenched tight, shaking them at Abe. "Can't you see?..." she wailed. "...My God, can't you see it?" She pounded her fists against his chest. "No... No... No!" Trembling now, Sara cried out, "My *father* is *the Beast*... My *father* is *the Beast*, and he doesn't even know it..."

Sara collapsed onto the carpet, undone.

Abe's jaw dropped. As always, Sara was light-years ahead of him.

Abe knelt beside her. Gently, slowly, he helped her back into the chair, then gave her tissues. As her crying subsided, he put a big hand on her shoulder. "Sara...Sara..." he softly said. "I had no idea...none... how...my god, how do you know this?" Abe waited while Sara took slow breaths, wiped her eyes. He brought her a cup of water, then a wet washcloth that she lay on her forehead. Abe took a slow breath too—it made sense: this was her horrifying knowledge.

Sometime later, when she was finally ready, Sara nodded at Abe. "Okay...okay...last summer, when Peter left without even saying goodbye, I knew the Beast had risen..." Another sip of water. "I didn't get how I knew that until just now...yes...yes...I could smell the Eucalyptus, the menthol...the cold cream...he'd come check on me at night, and in the morning I could still smell cold cream...I smelled it, faintly, in the car, when he drove me to school..." She took several slow breaths. "Then it went away for a long time... Just before they found Snapper's body, it happened again... One morning I smelled the Beast... Jesus, I'd bet it was my father in London, wearing makeup to look like someone else..."

"Of course, you use cold cream to remove makeup... Sara you're so damn smart..."

Abe's cell phone rang. "Can you see him?... Save it Lou...give me the address..." Abe wrote it down. "We'll be there right away." Abe turned off his phone, turned to Sara, "Your dad's at some kind of guest house on Capitol Hill. Lou can have a man come here and wait with you, but I'm thinking you'll want in on this."

"I have to go with you. And I'll stay with you, until we find Peirithous. It's more important now than ever. You understand that don't you?"

"Yes, Sara, I do."

"Uh, doc..." She took a moment—long slow breaths, a drink of water—then she pointed a forefinger at Abe. "You...*you're* my modern-day Theseus…it took me a while to get that." She nodded, took his offered hand. "Let's go get Randy." They flew out the door.

♦♦♦

In the lab, Minos was putting on his makeup. His makeup appliance was already glued seamlessly over his face. His curly-haired wig rested naturally on his head. He faced the mirror, putting on the final touches, covering his grotesque, reopened scar with the purple bloom that spread across his cheek.

As he finished his purple birthmark, his mind was racing and he was crazy mad, Cretan Bull crazy mad. Though the Master didn't understand yet what had to be done, Minos, the Cretan Bull, certainly did. Sara had to be heavily medicated and institutionalized, right away. She was just too close, and her credulity had to be compromised. The Cretan Bull would never hurt Sara. Ever. That would destroy the Master. Still, to protect the Master, she had to be marginalized. But Abe Stein, the Jew troublemaker, was another matter altogether. The Meddling Jew had to disappear— like the Devil Whore, gone forever. But first, Randy's body had to be presented. Minos wheeled the cot into the lab.

That's when the door flew open and Lou, Abe, Corey and Sara burst in. Lou's gun was drawn. In that instant, Minos knew—in the way a salmon knows where it's born—that the Master's life was over. He stared out the window, aware that there was one thing, one very important thing, left to do. He had a new feeling then. It washed over him, soothing on the inside. A tear ran down his cheek, seeping along the edge of the purple stain.

He turned to Sara.

Sara screamed, one long, desolate wail.

♦♦♦

Without fanfare, Lou handcuffed Minos' hands behind his back. "Nice," he remarked when he saw, up close, the finely-detailed makeup appliance that transformed his face, then he read him his rights.

Abe was already checking out Randy, who was unconscious, sweating but still breathing, barely. His "death mask" made him unrecognizable. It was very like the mask that Jim wore—only even more grotesque because Randy had no purple birthmark to cover his reopened scar. Abe looked closely at the ghoulish reopened scar, then he gently removed the makeup appliance. "Lou get an ambulance, and call your ME. Have him meet the ambulance at the hospital. Will he know what to do?"

Lou was already on the phone, passing on Abe's message. He turned to Abe. "You're not the only smart doctor in Seattle. He's got the antidote—atropine—and Saul says we've likely got two to six hours from the injection, depending on dosage. He's on it."

With Corey's help, Sara undid the straps tying Randy down, then she held his hand. She stared at Minos, silent now, though she was plainly distraught. Tears flowed down her cheeks. Corey brought over a wet washcloth that she set on Randy's forehead, then she put her arm around Sara, gently comforting her.

Minos took it all in, off somewhere.

"How long has the poison been in his system and what's the dosage?" Abe asked Minos. When he didn't respond, Abe said, forcefully, "Whoever the Hell you are, this is urgent."

Minos smiled, then in his little-boy-sing-song voice, "Eenee meenee minee mo...unlucky Red is dying...go boy go..."

"If you answer, I'll put in a good word for you with the judge," Lou offered. "And doctor, you're gonna need that."

"The doctor isn't here, officer. Minos is here," Minos said, defiant. Proud.

"Who are you?" Sara asked, still crying.

"I take care of your father," Minos replied to Sara, soft-spoken now.

Sara wiped away a tear with the back of her hand, but she didn't stop crying. "Does he know about you?"

"No, of course not."

"But you know about him?"

"Everything."

"Do you really want to take care of the doctor?" Abe asked. He was starting to get this, and it was mind-boggling, even for him.

"Yes, yes I do," Minos replied. His tone turned coarse, "Meddling Jew bastard."

Corey was in his face. "Watch your mouth, you miserable freak."

Minos glared at Corey. "I could squash you, like a filthy cockroach." He made a quick crushing motion with his fist.

Corey stepped back when Abe persevered. "If you really want to help the doctor, do him a very big favor—tell us how long ago you gave Randy the injection, the dosage, and anything else you put in his system."

"Please," Sara added. "Please, for me."

Minos turned to Sara, considering this. "For you..." He tilted his head toward Sara, a little bow. "An hour more or less. Cerberus' foam, wolfsbane. Thirty milliliters of tincture and a sedative."

The sirens wailed outside and the paramedics came rushing in. Abe explained that Randy had been poisoned, thirty milliliters, and sedated, that he needed close monitoring of blood pressure and cardiac rhythm and that Saul, the medical examiner, would meet them at the emergency room. Saul, he explained, knew the poison and had the antidote. They wheeled the body into the ambulance.

"So now you know," Minos mused.

"I know that Sara was right about *the Beast,* that Jim Peterson created another person to do his dirty work. I don't know why," Abe said.

Minos ignored Abe. "Would you like to know why?" he asked Sara.

"Everything," Sara softly said, between her tears.

"I am Minos. I am Minos, the Cretan Bull, son of Zeus, the Thunderer..."

Minos watched Sara, who leaned in, squinting, plainly interested.

"Your father never told you about his childhood on Crete, about his babaka, his father, Minos, the Cretan Bull, did he?"

"No."

"For reasons that will become clear, I can finally tell you now about your father's childhood and about your grandfather. I'd like to ask, though, that what you learn here today will be our secret, forever."

"I don't know if I can agree to that," Sara said, distressed now, edgy. And then, "You...agh! You're a monster...you're *the Beast!* You killed my friend." Sara was hanging on by a thread.

"A request is all—to protect your father. Listen, then you can decide. As for your friend, I had no choice...he was blackmailing the Master."

"The Master?"

"Your father."

"You are my father wearing some kind of fancy, freaky mask." Sara cried out angrily.

Minos shook his head, no, then again. He stepped closer to Sara. "It's complicated, but no, I'm not your father. Please remember that. Now give me a moment to regroup, then I'll tell you your father's shocking, tragic story. I would like to do that, for your father and for you. Minos sat at his lab table, staring down at the scrapbook, open to the last two photos of the Cretan Bull. He was readying himself, oblivious to the people watching him.

Corey stepped over to the lab table, inspecting the elaborate makeup supplies, the sophisticated tools. Lou came up beside her. "This is a true Logan-Stein classic, maybe your best crazy show so far—"

"Calm down, Lou," Corey cautioned.

"This is right up there with Nick, the two-faced, scumbag Season, and twisted Teaser aka mad-dog Loki... At least Teaser remembered what was happening to him, after." Lou pointed at Minos, still staring at the last two photos in his scrapbook. "This was Doctor Jim Peterson. I followed him here, watched him putting on his fancy makeup appliance. What is going on here? Who in hell is he now?"

"I'm guessing that, at the moment, he's his own father." Abe explained. "And I'm guessing that Minos, the Cretan Bull, wants to tell Sara about his son, Jim."

"Uh-huh...of course...should I arrest him, take the damn makeup off, then go to the station to take *Dr. Peterson's* statement?"

"I'm pretty certain that Jim Peterson doesn't know about Minos, the Cretan Bull, that he believes his son, Peter, is alive and well in Greece, that Dr. Peterson won't have anything new to add, no statement to make. If we ever want to know what really happened here, I think we should take the cuffs off, and let Minos tell it now, his own way. I don't think he's a threat to anyone, anymore."

"Something tells me I should follow your lead on this puppy." Lou cracked a knuckle. "You're my favorite shrink, ever."

"Mine, too." Corey smiled. She was still comforting Sara.

Lou took the cuffs off.

Minos stood, stretched his arms, then curled his fingers into horns at his temples.

"Let's start at the beginning then, Minos," Abe softly said, when Minos finally lowered his fingers.

Minos spoke to Sara. "Your father, who you know as Jim, was originally named after his own father. His given name was Minos. At five, your father, young Minos, saw his father kill his beloved half sister, Ariadne."

"I never even knew my father had a half sister," Sara said.

"Of course you didn't." Minos' tone was kind.

"His father, who he hated for killing his sister, was a boxer called The Cretan Bull. He died in the ring in Seattle, four years later, when the Master was nine."

"I thought my grandfather died on a fishing boat that went down in the Cretan Sea."

"No, he was an aging fighter who was literally beaten to death. Your father was there; he saw it." Minos let that sink in. "Soon after, the Master was sent to an orphanage. He was so very bright and able that he was singled out for a prominent Seattle family, the Petersons, who were looking to adopt. They didn't want to know the details of his past, and they changed his name to James Peterson."

"Yes, the Peterson's were my grandparents. We went every year to visit their graves."

Abe, Corey, even Lou, were mesmerized. There was something unexpectedly touching about Minos telling Sara her father's story. Abe sensed that Minos wanted Sara to know, to understand.

"The next years you know—how your father went to Lakeside, then to the U, then on to medical school at Yale. He met your mother, Niki, at Yale, where she was a widowed graduate student with a young son, Peter. Niki was studying ancient European history, specializing in Classical Antiquity in the Mediterranean region." Minos spoke slowly, deliberately, getting every detail just so for Sara. "They married when he was twenty-eight, came back to Seattle where she became a professor of ancient European history, and your father, Jim, became a popular doctor. It's important to remember that he had buried his past, driven it from his mind, his memory, totally. He didn't even know that he once spoke fluent Greek; he couldn't speak the language today, even if he wanted to. Jim became a selfless doctor, above the fray, idealized by his patients, paternalistic, always in control, rarely showing his feelings."

"Yes, I always wondered how anyone could be so detached, so calm when facing hard things. My mother could be very emotional."

"Yes, your father loved that about her. She reminded him of his wild and beautiful half sister, Ariadne, though he never told her that. She never knew about his true father, the Cretan Bull, nor about his family history in Crete. Being with her, and raising young children, was his happiest time. You were born when your father was thirty. Niki loved the Greek myths, which she'd studied—"

"Yes," Sara interrupted. "She studied European history. The very name Europe is said to come from the myth of Zeus, as the Cretan Bull, abducting Europa to Crete."

Abe thought Minos almost smiled. "Your father also knew the myths, from his father, though he didn't remember learning them. Somehow it was the only thing from his early childhood that he retained. Sharing them with you and Peter was a safe way for your father to share his past with his children."

"I remember those years as a very happy time for me," Sara confirmed.

"But six years later, tragedy struck again, in Greece."

"You mean we found out that my mother had cancer."

"Yes, and when she died soon after, in London, your father was beside himself, broken. He was unable to handle this loss."

"And that, I'm guessing, is where you came in," Abe said.

Sara put it together. "It was you dancing with another man in my hotel suite that night, wasn't it?"

"Yes, child, after Niki died, your father was devastated, overwhelmed. He wanted other men, an intense feeling that, at the time, Jim simply couldn't bear. So I appeared, briefly, for the first time."

Sara stared at him, rapt.

"Please remember that Minos, the Cretan Bull is nothing, nothing like your father. Jim is handsome; the Cretan Bull is disfigured. Jim is selfless, unexpressive, kind and passive; the Cretan Bull is ruthless, passionate, strong and decisive. As the Cretan Bull, I could take care of your father, protect him. And I could do what he really wanted when that was too hard for Jim."

"So it began in London, where Jim would make himself up and seduce other men?" Corey asked.

"Yes. Jim always liked making himself up. As a child, young Minos sat in his father's corner during his fights watching his trainer tend to his many cuts—brow, nose, lips, face and so on. That's when he first became interested in makeup. Later, he'd watch his father use makeup to cover his scars. As a teenager, in Seattle, he worked summers in a shop that sold special effects makeup to TV, Halloween masks, and foam latex appliances. Before he finished medical school, Jim was already a skilled makeup artist. In London, Sara saw a younger version of Jim's father, the Cretan Bull, my debut."

"But after London, you disappeared for a long time." Abe noted, aware that Minos was gently giving Sara her father back.

"For the next seven years, the Master didn't need me. He'd have the occasional affair with a young man, which he'd learned to manage, but mostly, he'd lose himself in his work."

"You came back the year Peter left, didn't you?" Sara asked.

"Yes, I did. And this is the hardest part of your father's often tragic life. As you know, Peter was wild, smart, ready for anything and unafraid. At seventeen, he sensed that Jim, his stepfather, was gay. For Peter, it was irresistible. He teased him, and as only Peter could do it, he seduced

Jim. For Peter, this was just an adventure, and when he met Snapper, he moved on. For Jim, it was something more. It was both unthinkable and unthinkably exciting. Jim confronted Peter and Snapper. Peter and Jim argued heatedly. In a rage, Jim slapped Peter too hard. Peter fell back and split his skull on the fireplace mantel. He died instantly. It was Jim's worst nightmare: a father killing his own child.

Corey missed a breath. "The same thing his own father had done to his half sister."

"Exactly. Nothing could have been worse for him."

"And Minos came back to take care of him," Abe suggested.

"Yes, truly, a more regular presence." And to Sara, "After Peter died, your father was incapable of functioning and things had to be done. Minos took care of everything. He disposed of the body. He paid Snapper off, sent him to California. He arranged a trail for Peter, for the postcards, and so on." His tone was matter of fact. His manner, considerate.

"Only Snapper came back and wanted more money from Jim," Corey speculated. "And by then, you were up and running, ready to handle whatever for 'the Master.'"

"Yes, by then, I knew exactly what to do. Though, as I started taking care of the important doctor, protecting him, I also started evolving. Soon I had a life of my own. I knew what had to be done for Jim and I did it. What I never saw coming was that I began having Jim's childlike fantasies, his childhood memories. I became a safe harbor for thoughts and feelings that, as Jim, he couldn't bear. I was both his father, the brutal, hard-hearted Cretan bull, and playful, sweet, young Minos before his sister died. And finally, the injured and angry young Minos in Seattle, watching his father fight and eventually die."

"How did you manage that?" Abe asked.

"It took a while to get the hang of it. Though the Master never acknowledged me, I experienced him as judgmental. In my mind, Jim could be angry with me or impatient. As Minos, I had all of Jim's early memories but also his awareness, after his father, the Cretan Bull, died. So I imagined what the Master would want, what would make him proud—Cretan Bull for protection, for ruthless, efficient elimination of all threats, for keeping his made-up world intact…young Minos for pleasing, for playing…"

Sara nodded, riveted. "You said that young Minos hated his father for killing his half-sister, Ariadne."

"Yes, he routinely imagined him in Hades, more specifically Tartarus, where he was tortured mercilessly by the Furies—in perpetuity."

Sara looked at Minos. "The hideous Furies with tears of blood dripping from their eyes and snakes for hair, wielding their brass scourges, three-headed Cerberus, the ferocious Hell hound, the child-eating Minotaur… My father wanted me to know about these things—the myths, the monsters, the heroes, everything. There had to be a reason."

"As you've looked for Theseus, I've thought about this, tried to understand it. With hindsight, I think that without knowing it, the Master was trying to warn you and Peter about—perhaps even prepare you for—the Cretan Bull. He taught you about his past in the only way he could. The harsh realities, the curses, the terrible punishments, the tragic outcomes in the myths were cautionary—why else would a parent encourage his six-year-old daughter to learn about the Minotaur, about Pasiphae and the Cretan Bull, about Centaurs ravaging Lapith women, about drunken, rampaging Maenads taking Pentheus for a wild beast and ripping him limb from limb. Why encourage his young daughter and son to learn about these monstrous things—unless, on some level, he feared that the coldblooded, murderous Cretan Bull might not be buried—or trapped in Tartarus—forever. When Peter left without a word, it triggered an internal warning system, and you relentlessly pursued him into the past. You rightly identified the Beast and tried to raise Theseus, that is to say, Peter. Your brother, Peter, didn't come to imagine he was Theseus by himself. He was raised to be fearless, to be the one person who could stand up to the Cretan Bull. What you couldn't know was that he'd been killed. But you, too, were raised to fight the Beast."

"Moira…Moira," she repeated. "I knew I had to stop the Beast."

"Yes, at least in part, that was your father's gift to you." He nodded.

Sara shook her head. "I never put that together."

"You should also know, Sara, that you were never in danger from what you called *the Beast*. The Master loved you, so you were never, ever, in harm's way."

"I didn't understand that either."

"Of course not. I wish I could have told you, but I couldn't reveal myself to you. And I never could tell you what I'm telling you now—it literally wasn't possible—while your father was alive."

"Aren't you going to become my father again?"

"No. I'm sorry…your father is gone, forever."

Minos turned, opened the scrapbook, waved them over. He went through the pictures of the Cretan Bull—with his daughter, Ariadne, with young Minos on the boat, as a handsome young man, his first fight, later fights, then the picture before one of his last fights—Snapper's mask—the picture after his last fight, when his scar was reopened and he died— Randy's death mask—and finally the last picture in the book, the Cretan Bull in his coffin. This is the first time, he explained, that the Cretan Bull's purple birthmark appeared. Minos described how the Cretan Bull's face was so disfigured in his last fight that the mortician at the funeral parlor sewed up his ghastly reopened scar and, using makeup, created the purple stain birthmark to cover the hideous scar. Today, Minos looked just like the Cretan Bull lying in his coffin.

When they acknowledged, even admired, the likeness, Minos turned on his overhead halogens, touched up his birthmark, then stood in front of the mirror.

Minos stood and waited, poised. He raised his thumbs, his long forefingers and framed his face. When he felt steady, and easy, even silky on the inside, he began his slow, silent dance. Minos' fingers curled into fists, finding their marks in the air, uncurling again. His fingers moved deftly, making shapes in the air, until the extended forefinger of each hand settled just above his temples, curling forward. Then he swayed his body, graceful and deliberate. Twisting and turning, he began his Bull dance again. When he had everyone's attention, he put on his black suede fedora, tipped his hat to Sara, bowed, and then he gently kissed her brow.

Minos, the Cretan Bull, went back to dancing his dance—part pantomime, part Crane dance, part shadow boxing, part bull dance. He swayed, twisted and turned, arms and hands moving gracefully through the air, until he was facing the window, then, in one fluid motion, he threw himself through the window, into the steep, rocky ravine below.

Sara gasped, then she cried a piercing cry, a desperate, keening wail.

Lou and Corey flew down the stairs, angling back and forth down to the rocky ravine below. At the bottom of the ravine, Lou tried to find Minos' pulse, but it was too late. His neck was broken, and Minos was dead. Corey shook her head—no—an unmistakable message to Abe and Sara, watching through the broken window.

Abe helped Sara to the desk chair, where she sat, laying her head in her arms, sobbing inconsolably. Abe brought her a glass of water and a wet washcloth. He massaged her shoulders until her crying lessened, then he let her rest.

Sometime later, she stood and came to where he was standing, looking down through the broken window, watching Corey help Lou take photos of Minos/Jim. When Abe saw Sara, he put an arm around her. "Sara, Sara… I'm so very sorry for your losses…it's more than I can imagine…" He held her close for a moment before offering, "But I know you, and though you may not believe this now, I know that before too long, you'll be able to move on…"

Sara pressed her thumb and forefinger to the bridge of her nose, crying again. "How is that possible?" she eventually asked, barely a whisper.

"You'll need time and a different kind of patience…and you'll need to draw, yet again, from your uncommonly deep well of courage…"

She took a calming breath. "It feels like way more than I can bear…"

"You're a strong, resilient young woman with a splendid mind. You'll grieve, you'll be very sad, but little by little, you'll learn to live your life again… I promise you that."

"Will you help me?"

"Of course I will."

Sara leaned into him. They looked out the broken window down into the deep ravine below for a long, long time.

◆◆◆

When Lou and Corey turned up the staircase that angled back and forth up the side of the ravine, Abe and Sara were still standing side by side, looking out the window. Sara turned to him, took another measured breath. "It would help me to talk about all of this," she gestured with her hand to include the lab, the ravine, everything. "Un-huh."

"I'm not sure what to say, Sara, and as you know, it's rare for me to be speechless."

She looked at him. "I understand. I feel the same. It's unreal... unbelievable."

"Yes, this is an unimaginable story. But I believe that everything Minos, the Cretan Bull, told you is true."

"Except that part about Zeus being his father, though I understand what he meant..." The corners of her mouth turned up just barely.

Abe nodded, pleased. "It confirms something that I've learned— Sara, you're a remarkable young woman. I think Minos, your father, Jim, and even the Cretan Bull were all immensely proud of you. Beyond words. You were right and unstoppable. Whatever was thrown at you, you wouldn't be derailed. I think, at the end, even the cruel Cretan Bull wanted you to know your father's story, to understand him, to love him in a way that Jim never loved his own father. He wanted that for your father, but he also wanted it for you. At the end, I think he was less Cretan Bull, more Minos—that is to say, what young Minos would have become if Jim hadn't suppressed his memories. And I think, after everything, the last thing, the final thing, that Minos, the Cretan Bull, could do to protect your father was to take his own life."

"He was wrong, though, like Aegeus, throwing himself off the cliff when Theseus forgot to put up his white sails."

"Yes, Theseus was still alive."

"Tragically. And yes, after hearing Minos' story, I was ready to forgive, and to love, my father the man, and to love young Minos, my father as a boy. Only the Cretan Bull had to die."

"And sadly, that was impossible."

"I don't think my father ever wanted to hurt anyone."

"I think you're right about that, Sara."

She was crying again. Abe put his arm around her.

They stood at the broken window. Abe tried to imagine what this was like for Sara. He couldn't. They watched Lou and Corey climb the long zigzagging steps. About half way up, Lou answered his phone. He raised a thumb in the air. "Randy's okay…he's okay," he yelled up at them.

Sara buried her face in Abe's chest and shoulder.

When she came up for air, a slow soothing breath, Abe said, "It's over Sara, you saved Peirithous… Yes, *you* did that… And *the Beast* is dead."

"Dear God, a real-life Greek tragedy…but yes, *the Beast* is dead… Moira…" She paused, grave, mulling something. After a long moment, she asked, tentatively, "Do you think all three of them were *the Beast*—my father Jim, Young Minos, and the Cretan Bull?"

"I was just thinking about that. This is complicated, and, I think, counterintuitive. But no, I think that they were three different people, inhabiting the same body. Three distinct, unintegrated personalities—at least until the very end, when Minos was telling you Jim's story. I think Minos, at the end, was Jim with all of his memories. You were right, though, if it were possible, only the Cretan Bull had to die. He was *the Beast*."

Sara nodded. "I think young Minos was a sensitive boy who became a caring man, in spite of all of the horrible things that he'd seen. He simply buried them." She made a sad face.

"If I may say so, young lady, that's no psycho mumbo jumbo."

"Thank you for that, my tireless therapist, my foul-weather friend, my modern-day Theseus…*you* saved my life."

"Truthfully, you gave me much more than you ever got from me."

"That's true, Sara." Corey was there, just behind them. "You reinvented his idea of himself as a therapist. I watched that happen." And taking their hands, "I know how you feel though, Sara. He saved my life, too."

EPILOGUE

(ONE MONTH LATER)

Billy, Amy, Sara, Randy and Alex were at their usual spot against the far wall of the Blue City Café. They'd gathered after a memorial ceremony for Peter at Waterfront Park. From Snapper's sketch of the gravestone, Lou Ballard had finally found Peter's grave in a pauper's graveyard. Sara had spoken, and after, they scattered Peter's ashes at sea.

"You took my breath away," Billy said to Sara. "I didn't really know Peter and you made him come to life for me."

"Thank you." Sara was wearing a simple black dress and beautiful pearls, left to her by her mother. The spiked collar was gone. She looked lovely. Sara had been living with Amy and her mom, and she and Amy had grown close.

Dave and a group of the popular kids came by. They were good-looking, thin, stylish—thoroughbreds. Dave came to their table. "How are you, Sara?" he asked her, apparently friendly.

Sara hesitated, wary.

"You okay?" Dave wanted to know.

Amy nodded, encouraging Sara to respond.

"Better. Way better." Sara said, tensing up, readying herself for she-wasn't-sure-what.

"I'm glad you're back in school," he said, matter of fact.

"Thanks."

Dave nodded then followed his friends to another table.

"What's that about?" Sara asked. "Why was he so nice to me?"

"Amy gets the credit for that," Billy explained.

"It was Billy's idea, too."

"What? When? Tell me," Sara implored, almost bubbly.

"Okay. Amy and I sat down with Dave and his super popular girlfriend, Marcie, last week." Billy offered.

Amy made a grim face. "Made Dave an offer he couldn't refuse."

Billy smiled just thinking about it. "So Amy explains that unless he and his friends start treating you nicely, respectfully..." Billy raised both palms. "And I am not kidding about this part—Amy tells them, in that serious way that only she can do it, how we are going to infect one popular girl a week with this aggressive, cystic acne—she even named the bacteria. Hideous pimples, inflamed lesions, nasty red blotches all over her face. Starting with Marcie, Dave's new babe."

"Get outta here."

Amy jumped in. "Billy had this petri dish—he said it contained a culture of acne inducing bacteria. He told them that *Acne Vulgaris* is the disease most commonly associated with what's called *P infection*. He even showed them some disgusting pictures he'd found online."

"Oh my god. How were you going to do this?"

"We did some research on drug-induced acne. We focused on drugs that could be orally administered, then we made up a very convincing story about this powerful, virtually undetectable, infectious solution. How no one would ever know or be able to prove anything."

Amy smiled. "One a week until he cleaned up his act."

"Dave began to argue. Amy shot Marcie a chilling look—*I will do this to you, believe me, honey.*" Billy went on, "That's when Marcie lay down the law with Dave. 'This is not happening to me,' she declared. 'Never. No fucking way!'"

"'Fuck them,' Dave said to Marcie. 'They're pussies. They wouldn't dare.'"

"'Try me,' Amy said. 'Sara's been through hell. Her father and her brother are dead. She's shown remarkable courage. She held her ground when nobody would listen to her. She saved Randy's life and likely other lives. She's had enough trouble. I promise you I won't stand by and watch her being harassed and bullied. Dave, you may get me back, you may try and bully your way through this, but *I goddamn guarantee you* that whatever else happens, Marcie's face is going to look like a pepperoni pizza—for a long, long time. And then Julie, and then maybe Josie, and so on until you back off and treat Sara respectfully. All of the time.' She turned to Marcie. 'Am I clear?'"

"Marcie turned to Dave, livid. I'm waiting for that freezing cold, dry-ice steam to come out of her mouth, her ears, her nose." Amy smiled. "When she finally spoke, Marcie spit out her words, almost hissing, 'You are not giving this crazy bitch and her low-life, ex-juvie boyfriend any excuse—any damned excuse at all—to mess up my face.' She planted a forefinger on Dave's chest. 'Clean up your act, hot shot, starting right now, or I tell all of the girls that you're cut off. No sex. Period. Not even a hand job.'" Amy squealed. "I am not kidding; she said that, then she pumped her fist." Amy nodded. "Yes, it's true." Sara's eyes were tearing from suppressing her laughter. "Then Marcie found Dave's eyes. 'Am I clear?'"

"Dave looked like he'd been gut shot. 'Hassling Sara's lame anyway,' Marcie added. She waited until he nodded, then she took his hand and led him out."

"You guys are great. Exceptional!" Sara said. "It's like you threatened to lay this heavy curse on them. And you chose the perfect curse. Take it from me. Marcie would do anything—and I mean anything—not to have pimples."

The entire group was laughing, exchanging high fives, and generally enjoying themselves when Maisie walked over from the coffee counter with a latte. They'd been so engrossed in Amy and Billy's story that they hadn't seen her come in.

She'd been at the memorial service, but kept to herself at the back edge of the group. When she set her latte down at their table, Billy stood to give her a big hug. She responded warmly.

"Hey, guys," Maisie said to the others, then she sat.

"Good to have you back," Randy offered. Alex nodded agreement. Amy squeezed her shoulder.

"Took a while, but yes, I really am back. And I'm okay." Maisie had been kidnapped on Thanksgiving, less than a year ago, by Teaser, a brilliant, diabolical predator on a mission of vengeance. He'd taken her to punish her father, his former cellmate. When Corey and Abe rescued her, in the eleventh hour, she was so traumatized that she couldn't talk. Abe had been her therapist when she was kidnapped, and he'd been seeing her four, then three times a week, since she was rescued. Maisie had taken a year of home schooling and worked with Abe to get to where she was now. This was her first time out by herself.

"Sara, I thought what you said about Peter was very moving. I'm so sorry for your loss." Maisie raised her latte. "To absent friends."

Everyone joined in, cups raised, "To absent friends."

Sara watched Maisie, who seemed poised, even happy with herself.

Billy watched them both, realizing that these delightful young women were here, thriving, because of his mom and dad. His parents had sensed that Maisie was in danger long before anyone at Olympic would listen. Then when Maisie and Aaron were kidnapped, his mom and dad had got them back. And his dad had hung in with Sara when nobody else would listen. He'd believed in her and, between them, they'd saved Randy's life. And now, Sara—who had chosen to be an outcast, who had set fire to an Olympic restroom while trying to reach the Delphic Oracle—was turning into this striking, fascinating young woman, in spite of her terrible losses. Amy said she was becoming a true friend.

Billy was distracted when Sarah leaned in, whispered something in Maisie's ear. They conferred privately, then Maisie nodded, yes, smiling enthusiastically.

Maisie turned to Billy, "Please don't be embarrassed by this."

Billy frowned, confused.

Sarah raised her cup again, as did Maisie, then together they said, "To Dr. Stein."

Then together, "Dr. Abe Stein, the rumply shrink who brought two shit-outta-luck, half-dead gals back to life."

Everyone raised their cups high. Amy squeezed Billy's hand under the table.

Maisie went on, "Yes…and to Corey Logan, an example for those of us who hope, when the day comes, to be brave women." She set down her cup and held hands with Sara and Amy.

They all rose.

Billy was more than a little uneasy. It wasn't good for your friends to like your parents. Un-unh. He knew that much. They were, after all, parents. Still, he could feel his heart swelling with pride.

ACKNOWLEDGMENTS

The author would like to thank: Tyson Cornell, Jacob Epstein, Dorothy Escribano Weissbourd, David Field, Ruth Grant, Steve Grant, Brendan Kiley, Patricia Kingsley, Robert Lovenheim, John McCaffrey, Kate Pflaumer, Mike Reynvaan, Andrew Ward, Ben Weissbourd, Emily Weissbourd, Jenny Weissbourd, Richard Weissbourd, Robert Weissbourd, Laura Wirkman

OF THE 12 OLYMPIAN GODS*, THESE ARE FEATURED IN *MINOS*:

Zeus overthrew his Father, the Titan Cronus, and then drew lots with his brothers, Poseidon and Hades. Zeus won the draw and became the supreme god, ruling over all of the Olympians. He is the presiding deity of the universe, lord of the sky. His weapon is a thunderbolt. He is married to Hera and is known for his many infidelities.

Poseidon was given all water, both fresh and salt, as his domain. He is the god of the sea, earhquakes, storms, and horses. His weapon is a trident, which can shake the earth—hence, his nickname "Earthshaker." He is the most powerful Olympian god, after Zeus, and is said to be moody and temperamental. He is one of Theseus' fathers.

Hades had the worst draw and was made lord of the underworld, ruling over the dead. He was adamant about keeping his subjects in his domain and reserved his rage for those who tried to steal souls or dared to defy him. He imprisoned Peirithous in the "Chair of Forgetfulness" when he (along with Theseus) tried to take Persephone, Hade's wife, from the Underworld and make her his own wife. Peirithous stayed in that chair—bound by snakes, with no memory at all—in the Underworld forever. (Theseus was eventually freed by Heracles, but even Heracles couldn't free Peirithous, who'd so enraged Hades.) The Greeks never spoke Hade's name, afraid that it might bring death. His weapon is a pitchfork. He has a ferocious three-headed dog, Cerberus, who guards the gates to the underworld, never allowing anyone to leave.

Hera is Zeus' wife and sister. She is the patron of marriage and childbirth and takes special care of married women. Hera is known for her jealousy and acts of vengeance against Zeus's lovers and their offspring, including Heracles, who she tried, unsuccessfully, to kill as an infant. She sent two snakes to his crib, and Heracles killed them both.

Apollo is the son of Zeus and the Titan Leto. He is the god of music, light, healing, truth, and prophecy. Every day, Apollo harnesses his chariot and drives the sun across the sky. He is famous for his oracle at Delphi and no king, including Alexander the Great, would go to war without first consulting the prophetic deity of the Delphic Oracle. His tree is the laurel.

Hermes is the son of Zeus and Maia, a mountain nymph. He is the messenger of the Olympian Gods, the link between mortals and the divine. He is the guide for the souls of the dead to the underworld and the afterlife. He is known as a cunning prankster and a friend to mankind.

*Adapted from Greek Mythology, the 12 Gods of Olympus, http://www.webgreece.gr/greekmythology/olympiangods/

OTHER MYTHOLOGICAL FIGURES AND CREATURES IN *MINOS**

Theseus—the legendary hero of Athens: son of Aethra, daughter of Pittheus, king of Troezen. It is said that Aethra lay with the sea god, Poseidon, and Aegeus, the King of Athens, on the same night and thus, Theseus was a demigod with dual paternity. Theseus was the founder king of Athens, and one of the most popular heroes in Ancient Greece. Among other great feats, he killed the Minotaur in Minos' labyrinth in Crete, killed Phae, the monstrous, white Crommyonian sow, defeated the bandits and murderers on the land route from Troezen to Athens (Sinis, the pine bender, Periphetes, the club bearer, Sciron, who pushed travelers off a cliff to be eaten by a giant turtle, and others. In each case young Theseus killed them as they killed others). Theseus had the strength and courage of a hero but he was also intelligent, wise, and a true friend of the poor and the oppressed. As founder king, he unified the twelve scattered Attic settlements into the single entity that became Athens and led the government toward democracy. "Not without Theseus" was a popular Athenian saying.

Minos: the first King of Crete, son of Zeus and Europa. Minos made King Aegeus pick seven young boys and seven young girls to be sent as tribute, every lunar year, to Crete to be fed to the Minotaur, hidden in his Cretan labyrinth. After his death, Minos became one of three judges of dead souls at the gates to the Underworld. He cast the deciding vote.

Pasiphae: Wife of King Minos of Crete. When Poseidon sent Minos a beautiful white bull, Minos did not sacrifice it as he had promised. Poseidon, in a rage, inflicted Pasiphae with a passion for the great white bull, which ultimately led to the birth of the Minotaur, a monster, half-man and half-bull. Minos had the Labyrinth built to house the beast. Pasiphae possessed the powers of witchcraft and put a terrible curse on Minos for his many infidelities.

Europa: the mother of King Minos of Crete, a beautiful mortal woman, said to be the virgin daughter of Agenor, the king of Phoenicia. The story of her abduction by Zeus in the form of a white bull was a Cretan legend. It is thought that the continent Europe was named for her.

Peirithous: Theseus's best friend, prince of the Lapiths. Peirithous was adventurous and rash, and consequently, he was often in trouble. Theseus, his devoted friend, regularly came to his rescue.

Centaurs and Lapiths: The Lapiths were a Thessalian tribe in Greek mythology. In one account, Lapithes and Centaurus were twin sons of Apollo and the nymph, Stilbe. Lapithe was said to be handsome and a great warrior but Centaurus was deformed. In this version, Centaurus mated with mares, who gave birth to the Centaurs, strange creatures who had the head, arms and chest of a man but the legs and lower half of a horse. The Lapith king, Peirithous, invited the Centaurs to his wedding feast. After drinking too much wine, the Centaur, Eurytion, attempted to rape Peirithous' bride Hippodamia, dragging her off by her hair at their wedding party. It was the beginning of a ferocious battle, in which the Lapiths, led by Theseus and Peirithous, drove the Centaurs from Thessaly.

Furies (Erinyes): Three female goddesses of vengeance. They were created when the Titan Uranus, was castrated by his son, Cronus, and his genitals were thrown into the sea; the drops of blood that fell onto the earth created the Furies. They are said to have snakes for hair, coal-black bodies, and blood dripping from their eyes. They carry brass-studded scourges and torment their victims relentlessly.

Pan the Satyr: Pan was the son of Hermes and the Nymph, Penelope. He was the rustic Arcadian god of the mountain wilds, fields, hunting, shepards and flocks. Pan was depicted as a man with the horns, legs and tail of a goat, and with a long, thick beard, a snub nose and pointed ears. Though an ugly and shunned satyr, Pan was known for his sexual appetites. He wandered the hills and mountains chasing Nymphs. He seduced Selene, the moon goddess, by covering his hairy, black goat's body with a sheepskin.

Maenads: The female followers of Dionysus. Literally "the raving ones," they were typically depicted in a state of ecstatic, bacchic, frenzy—unstoppable dancing, drinking and playing. If a maenad stroked the ground with her Thyros (a staff crowned with ivy), it is said that a stream of wine would spew from the earth. When possessed by Dionysus, the maenads were believed to have extraordinary strength. It is said that when King Pentheus banned the worship of Dionysus, the Maenads of Thebes tore him apart (as portrayed in Euripides' play, *The Bacchae*)."

*My impressions of these mythological figures were drawn from the works of Robert Graves, Edith Hamilton, Mary Renault and myriad internet sources.

HISTORY OF THE MYTHOLOGICAL WORLD

This chronology lists events in mythology and legend with known events in history.

The mythological dates are generally estimates based on the internal evidence in the myths. I consulted several mythological timelines. I began with Marc Carlson's Timeline, then consulted The Chronology of Greece and the Greek Myths, Angelfire's myth timeline (most of the descriptions are taken from this timeline), and the works of Robert Graves, Edith Hamilton and others. There are often contradictory opinions about dates (I've seen Theseus' birthdate estimated at anywhere between 1273BC—1261 BC) and in those cases, I made my best guess.

2500 BC—CONSTRUCTION OF THE PYRAMIDS BEGINS IN EGYPT.

- Cronus the Titan, Zeus's father to be, castrates and kills his own father, Uranus, the primal god of the sky.
- Cronus, afraid he will be overthrown by his own sons as he overthrew his father, imprisons his children in Tartarus, the deep abyss in the underworld. (Later legends claim he swallows them and that they survived inside him until released by Zeus.)
- Zeus is born on Mount Ida in Crete (in later legends, his mother tricked Cronus into swallowing a stone in swaddling clothes rather than Zeus). His existence is kept a secret from Cronus, and Zeus is raised in a cave on Crete.
- Zeus learns his destiny to conquer Olympus, which became the dwelling place of the 12 Olympian gods.

- Zeus frees his siblings from Tartarus (or, in later legends, from Cronus' belly where they survived after he swallowed them).

2404 BC—BIBLICAL NOAH AND HIS FAMILY SURVIVE THE FLOOD IN AN ARK. ZEUS CONQUERS OLYMPUS AND TAKES HERA AS HIS QUEEN; CRONUS FLEES INTO EXILE. ZEUS AND HIS BROTHERS CAST LOTS FOR THE WORLD AS POSEIDON INHERITS THE OCEANS AND HADES TAKES OVER TARTARUS AND THE UNDERWORLD.

- Hermes is born. Hermes was the messenger of the Olympian gods and their link with mortals. He also guided all dead souls to the underworld and the afterlife.

2000 BC—THE ANCIENT GREEKS BEGIN WORSHIPPING THE OLYMPIAN PANTHEON AS GODS.

- Prometheus steals fire to give to mortals. Zeus, enraged, punishes him by chaining him to a rock with an eagle feeding daily on his regenerating liver.
- Hera brings Pandora to life to bring misfortune to mortal man for accepting fire.
- Pandora opens a jar she was warned to never open and a hive of demons are released spawning evil in mortal man from it.

1469 BC—HADES ABDUCTS PERSEPHONE, DAUGHTER OF ZEUS, AND MAKES HER QUEEN OF THE UNDERWORLD.

- Greek armies invade Phoenicia. Aphrodite joins the Olympian pantheon. Zeus, disguised as a white bull, takes the Phoenician princess Europa to Crete, where he seduces her and makes her Crete's first queen. Minos is their son.

1273 BC—THESEUS BORN IN TROEZEN

1270 BC—KING MINOS OF CRETE DEFEATS ATHENS AND FORCES THEM TO PAY A TRIBUTE OF SEVEN

YOUNG BOYS AND SEVEN VIRGIN GIRLS EVERY
LUNAR YEAR TO FEED THE MINOTAUR.

1268 BC—HERACLES FREES PROMETHEUS.

1252 BC—THESEUS KILLS THE MINOTAUR, AND RE-
TURNS TO ATHENS. WHEN HE ARRIVES, HE FORGETS
TO HOIST HIS WHITE SAIL. AEGEUS, HIS FATHER,
SEES THE BLACK SAILS, AND THINKING THESEUS IS
DEAD, HURLS HIMSELF FROM A CLIFF INTO THE SEA.
THESEUS CLAIMS THE THRONE OF AEGEUS.

1248 BC—HERACLES GOES TO HADES AND BRINGS
BACK CERBERUS, THE HELLHOUND. HE FREES THE-
SEUS FROM THE "CHAIR OF FORGETFULNESS" BUT
IS UNABLE TO FREE PEIRITHOUS, WHO'S CRIME OF
WANTING THE WIFE OF HADES FOR HIS BRIDE WAS
TOO GREAT.

1223 BC—HELEN OF TROY BORN IN SPARTA TO ZEUS,
DISGUISED AS A SWAN, AND LEDA.

1209 BC—ACHILLES BORN IN PHTHIA.

1194 BC—THE TROJAN WAR BEGINS. ACHILLES IS
ONLY FIFTEEN YEARS OLD.

1184 BC—ODYSSEUS SMUGGLES GREEK SOLDIERS
INSIDE A WOODEN HORSE INTO TROY AND
SUCCESSFULLY TAKES THE CITY.

1050 BC—SAMSON, DEFENDER OF THE ISRAELITES,
TOPPLES THE TEMPLE OF SAMSON DOWN UPON
HIMSELF AND 1000 PHILISTINES AFTER BEING
BETRAYED BY HIS MISTRESS, DELILA.

1000 BC—DAVID SLAYS GOLIATH AND BECOMES
RULER OF ISRAEL.

750 BC—ROMULUS AND REMUS ARE THE LEGEND-
ARY FOUNDERS OF ROME.

350 BC—PLATO FIRST RELATES THE STORY OF
ATLANTIS.

6 BC—JESUS CHRIST BORN IN BETHLEHEM, JUDEA
CONTROLLED BY THE ROMAN EMPIRE. HE BEGINS
THE FOUNDATION FOR CHRISTIANITY.